SUMMER CAT BLUES

Alison O'Leary

RED DOG
UK

Published by RED DOG PRESS 2022

Paperback ISBN 978-1-915433-20-6

Ebook ISBN 978-1-915433-21-3

www.reddogpress.co.uk

For Alice Euphemia Price

CHAPTER ONE

THE ROOM WAS dark, the shape of the furniture only barely visible. He glanced across to the small hooded figure seated on the upright chair in the corner, silent now and still. He hadn't needed to tie his hands and feet together but he'd wanted to. Somehow, it felt more professional. More business-like. Also, he'd enjoyed it. He thought for a moment. Was there anything else that he needed to do? He crept silently towards him and leaned over. He knew that his closeness was sensed. He could hear the change in the rapid shallow breathing beneath the hood. Now what was it that he needed to do? Of course. He flexed his fingers and moved closer. He needed to strangle him. Fastening his grip around the warm soft throat he began to squeeze.

Gasping, he kicked out and sat up straight. The sweat was streaming from his face and chest as he swung his legs out of bed and stood for a moment, trembling. He needed light and air. He needed to breathe. Still unsteady on his feet he teetered towards the window and drew back the curtains. With hands still shaking he unfastened the window catch and leaned out, feeling the sweat cooling on his body. Outside it was cold and still. The only noise was the early morning bird song as they twittered and fluttered into wakefulness. He listened for a moment, while he thought about his dream. It had been so vivid, so real. But what if he really did it? Was it such a mad idea? He felt his heart beat quicken. It would solve all his problems, that was for sure.

He gnawed at the side of his thumb, the shredded skin already red and sore from where he'd chewed it before, began to bleed. Not the strangling, no, he couldn't do that, tempting though it was. Just the kidnap. He'd need to involve Edward and Emily, he didn't think that he could manage it on his own, but if it worked it would be the answer to all his prayers. And anyway, it wasn't such a big deal. Just moving a person from one place to another for a short time, that was all. They weren't going to torture or starve him to death or anything. It was risky though, there was no doubt about that. It would need very careful planning. The practical details such as the ransom needed to be thought about as well. They would need to work out how it could be paid without it being traced back to them which in essence would mean cash. What if they asked for between one and two million? Was it possible to obtain that much in cash? Maybe they should ask for instalments. But then, that meant dragging the whole business out and increasing the risk. Perhaps an account then. But there were strict rules on money laundering these days. Any bank manager worth his or her salt would have raised eyebrows at that amount of money going into a new account. He'd have to give that one some thought.

The room, already cold, grew colder and he closed the window. Spring had arrived early this year, bringing with it cold bright days and chilly nights. It would be summer before they knew it and they would all be at Seton Manor for his father's birthday. He huddled into himself. There were other practicalities to think about too. How could they make sure that none of them were identified? And what sort of time scale would they be looking at? Jacob drew a small notebook towards him and began making notes. There was no harm in at least thinking about it.

CHAPTER TWO

EMILY STARED OUT of the taxi window. She loved her brother dearly but would Jacob never shut up? Her other brother, Edward, sat in silence as he had done since they had all met at the station. She closed her eyes, conscious of the sound of Jacob's voice knocking against her ears. Whatever was wrong with Jacob, it was clearly something big. He didn't usually carry on like this.

"I mean, really, the whole thing is a damned farce," Jacob continued. "All this playing at happy families. I had a good mind not to come this year, I can tell you."

Right, thought Emily. Of course you did. Like you were going to miss out on a chance to start oiling round Daddy. Although she had to admit that Jacob was no worse than the rest of them. They loved their father, of course they did. But each of them was conscious of his enormous wealth and even more conscious of the fact that it looked like great wodges of that wealth was going into his new family. And if she was honest, she wasn't above doing a bit of oiling around Daddy herself. Her creditors were getting to the end of their tether and the demands were starting to come in thick and fast. It had got to the point where she dreaded hearing the rattle of the letter box and was afraid to open her email. A wash of bitterness trickled through her. It shouldn't be like this. Everything had been so lovely to start with, she'd never really had to think about money. Daddy could always be relied on. Until he met bloody Bridie.

"And that's another thing," said Jacob, oblivious of the fact that nobody was listening to him. "All this money they're spending. The way they're carrying on, there'll be nothing left. And as for the house, what they've done to it is a downright disgrace. Seton Manor is our family home. As the eldest son, I should have been properly consulted, I should have been ..."

"We," said Edward, turning his head and interrupting him. "We should have been properly consulted. There are three of us, in case you hadn't noticed."

"Oh shut up, both of you." Emily felt a tiny pinprick of a headache start just behind her left eye. "We've been through all this before. There's nothing that we can do about it. He's totally besotted with her. All we can do now is stick together and keep on her right side. That's if we don't want to be cut out altogether."

The three of them fell silent as the taxi passed through the wrought iron gates and swept up to the imposing entrance of the grand Georgian mansion. Edward got out and looked around him, his face pulled into a sneer which did nothing to improve his sour expression. Emily glanced at him. He looked, she thought, ill. His face was pale and drawn and his usual good humour was completely absent.

"Look at it. Just look at it. A bloody holiday complex and spa," he said, spitting the words out. "And to think how poor Mummy's living."

"Well, at least they've invited us for Daddy's birthday again. It won't kill us to try to be civil."

Emily sounded resigned. She leaned forward and pressed her credit card against the contactless pad. Yet more piled on the cards but what did it matter? She couldn't pay them anyway and this was a mere drop in the ocean compared to the total that she owed. If this was the old days she would have been in debtor's prison by now and right at this moment that didn't seem like such a bad option. At least her creditors wouldn't be able to get to her. Not for the first time she regretted opening her craft and book shop. She had been so happy at the beginning. She had always loved sewing and reading, and combining the two and opening the shop had seemed more like a hobby than a business. She had barely paid attention to the day to day running, so immersed had she been in ordering beautiful fabrics and yarns and buying new books. If she wanted a day off she simply paid a local girl to mind the shop. So what if she had let some of her friends have things on credit. They would pay eventually, she knew. Although, she reflected, those same friends seemed to be fairly thin on the ground recently.

She tucked her credit card back in her bag and climbed out of the taxi. Their step-mother, a small woman with a tiny waist, a winsome smile and great curls of auburn hair tumbling over her shoulders, came down the steps to greet them. Clinging to her left leg was a small boy dressed in a sailor suit, one finger up his nose and a smear of chocolate spread across his chubby face. Emily made herself smile down at him while her blood curdled.

"How lovely of you all to come." Bridie leaned over and gently untangled the little boy from her legs. "Come on, Orlando. Don't be shy. Say hello to your brothers and sister."

IN HIS ROOM, Edward crossed to the window and stared out. So many memories of when they were children here. Climbing the apple trees, swimming in the lake, running away from the gardener when they'd been caught stripping the fruit from the raspberry canes. Endless summer days with picnics and croquet on the lawn with their mother. He could picture the scene vividly, even after all these years. His mother laughing, slim in her striped cotton dress, her thick chestnut hair swinging forward as she raised the croquet mallet, Jacob sulking because he was losing, Emily with her nose stuck in a book. And now it was a bloody holiday complex. What was worse, it wasn't even their bloody holiday complex. That little bitch had fallen on her feet all right, and there was nothing that they could do about it. His expression darkened as he thought of the conversation at the club which his father had joined as soon as he had received his knighthood.

Sitting in the opulent room with the big leather winged back chairs and portraits of long dead members glowering down on them, he had studied the flickering flames of the fire while he sipped at the single malt he held in his hands. He had listened to the sound of his father's voice with a growing sense of disbelief.

"So you see, Edward, I must make sure that Bridie is looked after. She is, as you know, a little younger than I am."

That, thought Edward, fighting the urge to suddenly laugh, must be the understatement of the century. Could the man honestly not see that he was being taken for a fool? He looked like her bloody grandfather.

"And of course, there was the divorce settlement and the continuing care of your mother to consider. We are all aware, I think, that she has something of a drink problem."

Edward dipped his head and took a swallow of whisky. That's right, you bastard. Bring Mother into it. Who could blame her if she liked a drink? She didn't have much else to entertain her. All she had got out of more than forty years of marriage and the raising of three children was a poxy cottage on the edge of the estate which at one time was occupied by the head gardener when Seton Manor had such a thing, and she didn't even own that. The pathetic little allowance you pay her is just about enough for her to live on while you're living at Seton Manor with

Bridie in the lap of luxury. That pathetic excuse of a lawyer that Mother had was barely out of law school, while you, with your team of hotshot city lawyers stitched everything up very nicely. But which one of us was going to challenge you on it? None of us. When it came to the bread we all knew which side ours was buttered. Even Mother had advised them to keep their heads down. He kept his face impassive as his father continued.

"And we must not forget that there is now Orlando to consider. It was Bridie's idea to turn Seton Manor into a business and I think that it is a good one. It will operate under the new company that I have formed. Naturally Bridie is a director."

And Edward had smiled and nodded as his heart turned black. The way their father had behaved in recent years had been bad enough. But this, the vandalising of the family home, was way beyond anything that any of them could have expected. Seton Manor had been purchased and renovated just after Edward had been born, although his father always tried to give the impression that it had been in the family for generations. It was the house that they had grown up in and it was the house that held happy childhood memories for all of them.

He had opened his mouth to speak and then closed it again. He knew from experience that it was no good arguing with the old man. Any attempt to argue or cajole would simply have met with a stone wall of resistance. Once his father set his mind on something, it remained set. He had been a successful man of business for good reason. Removing his glasses, he had held them up to the light before slowly polishing them with his handkerchief while he played for time. In truth, he had been struggling to contain himself. Perching his glasses back on his nose he had looked across at his father who was, he had to admit, not looking at all bad for a man in his seventies. Tall and broad with the square jaw and steely expression that none of his

11

children had inherited, he looked every inch what he was. Successful, powerful, and rich. A well cut suit hid the paunch which had started to develop, his even white teeth were the product of expensive dentistry and he was sensible enough not to colour his thick iron grey hair.

They had all known about his indiscretions before of course, although their mother had done her best to hide it from them. The long business trips, the unfamiliar scent that sometimes wafted in with him when he came home, it hadn't taken a lot of working out, especially when they reached teenage years and were more aware of such things. But Bridie… Bridie had come as a shock to everyone. Forty years younger than him and working as a barmaid in the local pub while she was doing what she called 'resting' from her usual profession of acting, she would have been the last person that any of them would have thought he had anything in common with. But then, he reflected, they hadn't needed to have anything in common. She had just needed to make him feel good. And she had. There was no doubt that she had seen his father coming though, and it hadn't been too long before he had been 'popping out for a pint' most nights of the week. It had hit his poor mother like an oncoming train. Whereas with his other affairs she had been able to simply wait it out, this time it was different. Bridie, with her tight little shift dresses and hair extensions, her long fluttering eyelashes and breathy little voice, was playing to win. And she had. While most people would agree that his mother was what was euphemistically described as well-preserved, as though she was an upmarket marmalade, she couldn't compete with Bridie. Very few could.

But he had to keep on Bridie's good side. They all did. They had no choice. Her influence over his father was undeniable and now she had that little shit Orlando as a bargaining chip as well.

He closed his eyes as he felt a prickle of sweat break out on his forehead. Only three months until the auditors arrived and then his goose would be well and truly cooked.

CHAPTER THREE

AUBREY YAWNED AND arched his back before settling back down and stretching his paws in front of him. It had been a good day today. He'd been down to the beach with Vincent, mucked about in a few rock pools and caused panic and chaos among the crab population, started to pick a fight with a seagull which he'd then had the sense to back down from, and then home for dinner. Rising up again he strolled through to the sitting room where Molly, Jeremy and Carlos were looking at some brochures. The early evening sun filtered through the window and cast a gentle glow over their bent heads.

"What about Aubrey and Vincent though?" asked Carlos.

Aubrey stopped in his tracks and pricked his ears. What about Aubrey and Vincent?

"Well," said Jeremy, "they'll have to go to a cattery, I suppose."

A what? Aubrey looked across at Vincent who was draped across Molly's feet and listening carefully while appearing not to.

"It's a sort of place where you can put cats," Vincent said. "When their owners go away. They put you in cages," he added.

Aubrey jumped onto Jeremy's lap. He didn't like the sound of this. He didn't like the sound of it one little bit. He'd been in a cage once before, when he was banged up in Sunny Banks rescue centre before Jeremy had sprung him, and he had no intention of being caught like that again. He nudged Jeremy's hand with his head and stared up at him with his big golden green eyes. Jeremy smiled and ran his hand down Aubrey's back.

"Don't worry, old chap. It won't be for long."

Aubrey settled himself more firmly on Jeremy's lap. It wouldn't be at all, if he had his way. If necessary, he'd feign illness. Although, on reflection, that might mean missing meals for a time which wasn't such a good idea. He'd talk it over with Vincent later. At their last house, on the rare occasion that the Goodmans went away, the girl across the road came in to feed them. Maybe they could do something like that here, too. As if reading his mind, Carlos looked up from the brochure that he'd been reading.

"Couldn't we just ask one of the neighbours to come in and feed them?" he said. "You know, like we used to do at the old house?"

Even as he spoke, Carlos realised that it wasn't really a viable option. The neighbour on one side was an elderly gentleman who was looked after by carers and frequently became confused as to which day of the week it was. On one occasion he had knocked on their door to ask which house he lived in. The neighbours on the other side were a couple who worked for one of the airlines. They were away more often than they were home.

"This one sounds promising." Molly pushed her glasses on to her head and tapped with one finger on the brochure that she had been studying. "Seton Manor."

"What is it?" asked Jeremy. "Is it a hotel?"

"It's a hotel plus apartments. It's got a pool and a spa and there's a nine hole golf course as well. It hasn't been open long. It looks like it's set in lovely countryside." She laid the brochure down on the small side table and looked across at Jeremy. He loved his work with Her Majesty's Inspectorate but there was no doubting that it was stressful and there were times when he needed to step away from it. The last inspection that he had undertaken had been particularly difficult and had resulted in both the head teacher and the deputy head resigning, an outcome which, while not only expected but desired, had nevertheless been distressing for everybody concerned. "Jeremy, I know that you're not that keen on going away but you need a break. We all do. We haven't been away anywhere since we moved here, not even for a long weekend."

Jeremy nodded reluctantly. Molly was right, but the problem with holidays was that they were a bit like those exciting looking boxes that you got for Christmas when you were a kid. A compendium of games or a magic set. Full of promise on the outside but when you opened them there were just a few bits of tatty card and plastic and some mad instructions that were impossible for the average eight year old to follow. Most holidays that he'd been on as an adult, he had been bored after the first day and secretly wanted to go home again. But it wasn't fair on Molly, he knew. She worked hard at Lilac Tree Lodge and some of the residents were more than a little demanding. She deserved a break.

Carlos picked up the brochure that Molly had laid down and began reading the description of Seton Manor. He looked up, suddenly excited.

"It says here that if you book one of the apartments you can take small pets by consultation. What does that mean? What's a pet by consultation?"

"It means that you have to talk to the owners first. It also means that you can't take your horse," replied Jeremy.

"So does that mean we could take Aubrey and Vincent?"

Jeremy looked across at Molly and raised his eyebrows.

"In theory, I suppose," she said. "But by small pet it really means dogs."

Carlos stuck his chin out, looking in that instant remarkably like his mother. Jeremy suppressed a grin. Carlos's mother, Maria, had been short, loud and quite mad. But she usually got what she wanted. Until she got murdered, he reflected soberly.

"But it doesn't say 'only dogs'. It just says small pets." Carlos jabbed at the page with his forefinger. "I mean, like, what if you wanted to take your hamster? Or a parrot?"

"Carlos," said Molly patiently, "we haven't got a hamster. Or," she added, "a parrot. Anyway, the cats might get confused. They like routine and knowing where everything is. They might run away if we take them to a strange place."

Aubrey raised his head and looked across at her. Run away? Fat chance. Both he and Vincent knew when they were well off. They both had all their paws well and truly under the Goodman table.

"And then there's the journey. They would have to travel in their baskets. In the car."

Aubrey thought for a moment. Which was worse? Car and basket or cage? Cage, definitely.

"Well then, just you and Jeremy go. I'll stay here and look after them."

Molly shook her head.

"No, you've worked very hard at college this year. You could do with a break too."

Although, if she was honest with herself, that wasn't the only reason. There had been too many stories in the press lately about teenagers having parties while their parents were away, with the result that the house got trashed. She had seen the tragic photographs of bewildered looking parents staring around at the chaos of broken furniture and smashed glasses, while their little darlings cried and swore that it was gate crashers. Carlos was a sensible boy, she had no doubt of that, but if the word got around that he was in the house on his own then who knew what might happen. It was a nice town that they lived in but, as with most places, there was definitely an undesirable element. And some of those undesirable elements attended the same college as Carlos.

"I'll ring Seton Manor. Let's see what they say about bringing Aubrey and Vincent. But," she added, "I'm not making any promises."

CHAPTER FOUR

CARLOS GLANCED DOWN at the cat baskets tucked in on either side of him. Inside both baskets a slumbering cat lay with its tail curled round and its head under its paws. It had been Molly's idea to ask the vet for something to calm them and although he hadn't been keen on the idea to start with in case it made them ill or something, he was glad now that she had. It was just a little spray thing but it seemed to have done the trick. Apart from an initial token protest, they had slept for most of the journey. In the front, his hands on the wheel, Jeremy sang softly along to some of his favourite 80's numbers.

For someone who wasn't keen on a holiday, Carlos reflected, Jeremy certainly seemed to have entered into the spirit of things. He'd even bought some new swimming trunks, kidding Molly that he'd purchased a pair of bright red Speedos before he relented and showed her the neat blue shorts that he'd actually bought. Next to him she slumbered peacefully, her small blonde head lolling sideways. She was tired, Carlos knew. There had been a number of staff shortages at Lilac Tree Lodge care home and, as manager, she had usually picked up the slack by working double shifts. If any of them needed a break, Molly did.

He turned his head and looked out of the window, watching the greenery of the countryside as it flashed past. It was an alien world to him and he would have been hard pressed to identify one kind of tree from another. It wasn't the kind of thing that they taught you at school, although he could probably identify a glacial landscape should they happen to run into one. This place they were going to was on the edge of a village though, and he did know a bit about villages. They had lived in one for a year when Jeremy was on exchange with another school, but he'd never really explored the surrounding countryside. Not properly. When he was younger and Maria was alive she had sometimes arranged trips on one of the rare days when she wasn't working. But it had always been to a museum or art gallery, somewhere that was free to enter, so that he could learn about this new country of his. The closest that they had got to open green space was a trip to the local park so that Maria could look at the flowers. He let his head rest back against the seat and closed his eyes while he thought about his mother.

England, he had known from a young age, had been Maria's dream and it was a dream that she had been determined to turn into a reality. She had worked hard and saved what little money she had until they could escape from the back streets of Sao Paulo and the life of poverty that they had been born into and make their way to England. The land where all their dreams would come true. And at the centre of it, the absolute core, the driving force, had been Maria's resolution that Carlos should make something of himself, whatever it cost her. Now he was older, he knew in his heart that her resolution would never have been enough. She hadn't understood the ways of society, and neither had he in those early days. It was, if he was brutally honest, only when he was fostered by Molly and Jeremy that his life had really changed.

While his mother had given him unconditional security and love, it was with Molly and Jeremy, with their understanding of how the world worked, that he had prospered. He had done well at school and he was doing well at catering college. They had encouraged his interests and shown him a different way of being.

His dream of owning his own restaurant didn't seem such a far off fantasy as it had once done. Not for the first time, he found himself wondering, if Molly and Jeremy hadn't taken him in, where would he be now? Not sitting in a comfortable family car on his way to a nice holiday with the beloved cats either side of him, that was for sure. More likely he would have been taken into care until he left school and then spent his time kicking round the streets and getting into trouble, maybe even joining a gang for protection. A brief interlude between leaving school and following the family tradition set by his father of being sent to prison.

Not, he thought, suddenly guilty, that Maria hadn't done everything that she could. But it was a fact of life that living as an illegal immigrant in a squalid flat, with even more squalid neighbours around them, was not a propitious start. Simply attending school in England was not enough either, in spite of Maria's absolute faith in all things British. Especially when that school was Sir Frank Wainwright's, best known for failing almost every Ofsted inspection that it had ever been subjected to. Jeremy had once said that the only reason the authorities didn't close it was because they would have to disperse all the kids. It was better to keep them in one place where they could see what they were up to.

But he would repay his mother's belief in him. He had vowed when she died that he would, and he had it all planned. He would work hard and pass all his exams. When he finished catering college he would get a job in a good restaurant, maybe several, and put in as many hours as he could to gain some proper experience, maybe he would even work abroad for a while. Paris perhaps, or somewhere edgy like Berlin. Then, when he was about twenty-five, he would open his own restaurant and call it Maria's. His chef's whites would have his name embroidered on them, probably in red because that had been his mother's favourite colour. People on the telly would eat there and he would be famous. And rich, so that he could buy a Mercedes for Jeremy and fur coats for Molly. Well, maybe not fur coats. Teddy wouldn't approve.

At the thought of Teddy he felt his heart give a tiny squeeze. Small, dark-haired with green and blue highlights, and extremely pretty, he had lost his heart to Teddy when they had first met and she and her brother Casper had been resident pupils at a local school, Arcadia Academy. Although the Academy had closed down, he and Teddy had kept in touch. This Seton Manor place was only about twenty miles from where she lived.

CHAPTER FIVE

JEREMY LET GO of the small case he was wheeling in front of him and stared around him. The apartment was actually far nicer and much more elegant than he had expected. In spite of having seen the pictures in the brochure, somewhere in his subconscious he had been anticipating a sort of holiday camp set up like the one his grandparents had taken him and his brother to when he was seven. His mother had been in hospital with some unspecified and not to be discussed complaint, and his grandparents had thought, correctly, that a little holiday would distract them. The holiday camp they had chosen had been a paradise for a seven year old. He and his brother been given their own cosy chalet with a little bathroom and twin beds. Their grandparents had been in the chalet next door and both boys had thought that it was exciting beyond belief to have their own little house with no grown-ups in it. Each morning they had made plans to stay up until after midnight and eat chocolate and play games. Most nights they were spark out by eight o'clock, worn out by the constant round of fun going on outside and the endless supply of adults in brightly coloured jackets who were willing to play with them. There had been a camp song, too, which they had all sung at mealtimes. If he thought about it hard enough he could probably sing it even now...

"What do you think?" asked Molly, breaking into his thoughts.

Jeremy nodded his head.

"Very nice." And it was. A proper apartment with two bedrooms and a beautifully furnished sitting room with a small kitchen set to one side, he couldn't fault it. He wandered through to the bathroom and stared at the marble floor and the huge roll top bath. He reached out and touched the fluffy white towels hanging on the heated towel rail next to the walk-in shower, which was at least twice the size of the one they had at home. This was like a luxury hotel. The photographs in the brochure hadn't done it justice. He strolled back through to the sitting room and smiled.

"More than nice. This is great," he said.

"Can I let them out yet?"

Carlos looked up from where he was kneeling on the carpet staring into Aubrey's basket and tickling him on the nose with an outstretched finger.

Aubrey yawned and stretched. That had been one good sleep. He could barely remember the journey at all.

"We need to get a few things set up first," said Molly. "We know that the owner wasn't that keen on having cats here. I had to really convince her that they were well-behaved. In the end she said that said that we could only bring them on the understanding that we would be completely responsible for them. And that starts with a litter tray."

Aubrey sat up straight. Litter tray? What did Molly think they were? Kittens or something?

"I'll do it. Where shall I put it?"

"Good point." Molly turned to Jeremy. "Where do you think?"

"Not the kitchen." Jeremy's tone was firm. He loved both Aubrey and Vincent dearly but a litter tray in the kitchen was something that he really couldn't contemplate. "What about by the entrance?"

"One of us might step in it when we come in," Molly objected.

"I'll put it in my room. I don't mind." Carlos, his eyes bright, reached for the big bag of cat litter that he'd hauled in from the boot of the car.

"Well I mind, Carlos," said Molly, wrinkling her nose. "You can't have a litter tray in your bedroom."

Jeremy smiled. A sense of smell was something that teenagers seemed to develop only when they got older. He remembered his own mother throwing open his bedroom windows while she hoiked out piles of socks and grubby football shirts from under his bed, and stared down in disbelief at the interesting mould that was growing in the coffee mugs lined up on the chest of drawers. To be fair, he reflected, Carlos wasn't too bad on that front. In fact he wasn't bad at all. He always put his washing in the linen basket and while it was true that he did sometimes eat in his bedroom, although Molly preferred that he didn't, he always took out any plates or mugs that he had used and put them in the dishwasher. Jeremy guessed that was probably down to training by Maria, that and having basic hygiene instilled in him on his catering course.

"What about the little balcony?" Jeremy pointed to the French doors. "They're pretty good at letting us know when they want to go out. We can put their food bowls out there, too."

The three of them turned and looked at the small balcony. Molly walked over and opened one of the doors. It was just big enough to take a couple of chairs and a small table. Below was a swimming pool, the cool blue of the water sparkling in the sunlight. Stretched out on one of the loungers lay a tall thin man wearing baggy green shorts, his straw hat pulled forward across his eyes. As she watched he was approached by another man and a woman who flopped down on the loungers either side of him.

The woman poked him in the ribs and he sat up, his expression irritable. Molly backed away through the door again. It looked like they were going to start arguing and she didn't want them to think that she was eavesdropping.

"What's that?"

As she spoke she moved across to the front door and picked up a small white envelope sticking through the letter box.

"It can't be a bill," said Jeremy. "We've only just got here."

Molly slit open the envelope and stared down.

"That's nice."

"What's nice?"

"It's the owner's birthday and everybody is invited for cocktails this evening."

CHAPTER SIX

AUBREY AND VINCENT emerged from the edge of the small shrubbery and looked around them. The jump down from the balcony had been easy and once they'd freshened up and eaten after their journey they were keen to explore.

"Seems all right here, Aubsie," said Vincent, glancing across at his friend. "Should find plenty to do."

Aubrey nodded.

"Better not be out too long, though."

There had been some discussion between Molly, Jeremy and Carlos as to whether they should be allowed out at all and in the end Aubrey and Vincent had solved it themselves by simply leaping off the balcony. He looked up. Molly was still watching them from the apartment, her expression tense. Jeremy had been more pragmatic, being of the opinion that if they went out they would be back again when they wanted feeding. Which, Aubrey thought, was rather hurtful. Although, he reflected, it did have an element of truth in it. In front of them, sitting at one of the little decorative tables ranged round the pool, three people were talking. Aubrey and Vincent looked at each other and then inched closer, sidling round the back so that they remained unseen. If these three were cat-friendly then they could be on to a good thing. There was no question that Molly and Jeremy wouldn't give them everything they needed plus quite a lot that they didn't, but on arriving at a new destination it was a cat's priority to explore, and then exploit, any opportunities.

"It's all right for you, Emily. You've got your little shop."

"Oh is it, Jacob? Is it all right for me?"

She looked at him and narrowed her eyes. What on earth was the matter with him? He had always been encouraging about her shop and often ordered books online from her as well as recommending them to his friends. Why was he now referring to it as 'little', as though it was some kind of plaything? She ran her eye over his prematurely lined face and thinning hair. As a young man he had been good-looking, handsome even. He had certainly set some of her friends hearts aflutter. But now he looked old, almost worn out. She sipped at her iced drink. She loved both her brothers dearly and certainly when they were children they had always watched each other's backs. But being the only girl, there was no question that she had been given an easier time of it than her siblings. While the boys were expected to be good at games, excel in all matters academic, and never cry, all she needed to do was look pretty and smile. But, she reflected more soberly, she needed to do more than look pretty and smile now. Since his marriage to Bridie and the arrival of Orlando, her father's wallet had remained more or less firmly closed.

At the thought of her father's wallet, she felt her spirits sink even further. The chances of it opening any time soon appeared to be remote to say the least. Perhaps she should tell Edward and Jacob about her problems? They might be able to come up with something. At the very least, it would be good to talk about it. She took a deep breath.

"Actually Jacob, it very much isn't all right for me. If you must know, I'm in debt right up to my neck. And the shop is making a loss."

Jacob stared at her.

"I thought that Father was bank-rolling you."

"Not since…"

"Bridie," Edward finished for her. "Well, if it's cards on the table time, things are none too good for me either."

This time it was Emily's turn to stare. Edward was a senior partner in what she had always thought was a successful firm of solicitors.

"Why…" she began stumbling over her words. "Edward, what's happened? Is it Delia?"

Edward shook his head and then laughed suddenly, a short barking noise that was shocking in its bitterness.

"No, it's nothing to do with Delia."

"Well, what is it then?"

"The usual sordid little tale."

"Been helping yourself to client funds, have you?" asked Jacob. "Been dipping your fingers in the till?"

Edward nodded.

"That just about sums it up."

Jacob looked shocked.

"I was joking, Ed. You haven't really, have you?"

"But why?" Emily sounded confused. "You earn loads don't you?"

"Not enough," said Edward.

Jacob groaned and shook his head.

"It's Delia, isn't it? All those skiing holidays. All your cleaners and gardeners. That house. She must spend thousands a year on her hair alone. And the school fees for the twins must be astronomical. Why didn't you bring her with you, anyway?"

"She's on a spa break with two of her friends. And anyway, she doesn't like Bridie any more than the rest of us. Why didn't you bring Felicity?"

"She didn't want to come," said Jacob simply.

"Anyway," Edward continued. "It doesn't matter how it's happened. The fact is that it has and I am well and truly up shit

ALISON O'LEARY

creek with a conspicuous absence of paddles." He paused. "The auditors are due in soon."

"Can't you put it back?" asked Emily.

Edward sighed and passed a hand over his eyes.

"If only. Of course, I always meant to. It was always just temporary. Just something to tide me over. The first time it didn't even seem that wrong. Just like a sort of loan. But the amounts got bigger and bigger and then before I knew it, I was out of my depth."

"How did you get it past the accounts department?" asked Jacob, curious now.

Edward looked at his brother, his expression bleak.

"More easily than you might think." He paused. "Quite a lot of my clients are elderly. Also, we manage trust funds."

"Does Delia know?" asked Emily. Even as she put the question, she knew the answer. Delia was one of the lilies of the field. She simply accepted what she was given as her right. The thought that someone might have had to work hard for it never seemed to occur to her. She wasn't unlikable, not like Bridie, but she had a sort of otherness to her which enabled her to drift through life without engaging with any unpleasantness. Edward adored her and would have given her the earth. Which presumably was how he had found himself in this position now.

Edward gave a wry smile. It was, Emily suddenly realised, the first time that she had seen him smile since they had arrived.

"What do you think?"

"What will the other partners do when they find out?" asked Jacob. "Surely they'll cover for you if you explain? I mean, you've been there for years. You're a senior partner, for God's sake."

Edward shook his head.

"No, they won't. And, to be honest, if I was in their position, neither would I. The best I can hope for is an honourable resignation with the proviso that I pay the money back. Which I can't. The worst case scenario is that they will report it to the police and then I expect that I'll go to prison."

Emily sat up straighter, the pain evident on her face. Edward, of all people, being in prison. She couldn't bear to think about it.

"Surely that can't be right. I mean, I mean..." she paused. What did she mean? "It's a first offence and everything. They won't send you to prison for a first offence."

"Yes, they will," said Edward. "All right, the fact that I haven't got a criminal record will probably go in my favour. But only in terms of how long the sentence is. The thing is, with something like this, it's not just a theft. It's not like I've nicked a bag of crips from the corner shop. This is a breach of trust. Both in relation to the clients and the other partners. The courts take a very dim view of it."

"But Edward, you must ask Daddy to help," Emily insisted, pushing back the rush of tears that threated to fall. "You must."

Jacob turned to Emily and reached for her hand. For all her grown up ways, she was still his little sister.

"Em, it's not Father that he needs to ask. Father will tell Bridie and even if Father agreed to bail Edward out, Bridie will talk him out of it. Look how she behaved when we suggested that Mother's allowance might be increased."

The three of them fell silent. Following a visit to their mother, they had decided, the three of them, to tackle their father over their mother's situation. Not that she was badly off but there wasn't much left to spare at the end of the month and certainly not enough for any luxuries like a holiday, whereas their father and Bridie were clearly living a very comfortable life indeed. They had, all three of them, offered to pay for anything that she wanted but their mother had always refused. At the time

Bridie had been all smiles and sympathetic nods but they had all known that as soon as they left the room she would be on to their father. They had made the case and then stood outside the door and listened as hard as they could, like the children they had once been.

As Edward had remarked afterwards, Bridie should have been awarded an Oscar for that performance. She had played her final card with such skill that even the three eavesdroppers had been half-convinced. Their father was all that she and Orlando had and Orlando was still such a small child. Who knew what the future might bring? Much of his money was held in investments. Elizabeth had been very well provided for and it would be foolish to give any more of it away. What would she do with it anyway? Only drink more gin. And what on earth did she need that she didn't have? Everybody knew that financial situations could change overnight. What if they lost everything? It would be so awful, she had said, if she was forced to go back and work in the pub. And there were so many men at the pub constantly bothering her, the pub being, she reminded him, where they had met.

Jacob stood up and stared out across the countryside, one hand shielding his eyes. On the other side of the pool Orlando stood watching them, his cheeks bulging with sweets and his stout little legs planted firmly apart. Jacob turned back to his brother and sister.

"We could always kidnap the little bastard."

CHAPTER SEVEN

MOLLY REACHED OUT and accepted the cocktail glass that the smart little waitress handed to her. She'd never actually had a cocktail with a paper umbrella in it before. She glanced across at Carlos who was studying the hotel menu with interest. She smiled. Carlos read menus like other people read novels. If she didn't keep an eye on him he'd be sneaking off to the kitchen to talk to the chef. By the big marble fireplace two golden retrievers slumbered, apparently oblivious to the people milling around in the room. She turned her head and looked at the little group clustered in the corner. They were the people that she had seen earlier by the pool. From the expressions on their faces, they all looked as though they rather wished that they were somewhere else. She turned back as a tall elegant man with thick iron grey hair approached her.

"Allow me to introduce myself. Sir William Pelham. And they," he waved a hand towards the group in the corner, "are my three eldest children. Come to celebrate my birthday with me."

Molly glanced across again at Sir William's three elder children. They didn't look like they were celebrating.

"Happy birthday," she said, and tilted her glass slightly towards him.

Sir William smiled.

"Ah, too many birthdays now to want to mark them. This evening is all Lady Pelham's doing, I'm afraid." And he turned towards the small woman with her thick auburn hair piled artistically on top of her head with an unmistakeable look of adoration. "Are you staying in the hotel or one of the apartments?"

"An apartment," said Molly. "It's lovely."

Sir William nodded gravely.

"Very kind of you to say so. Ah, here's my youngest son, Orlando."

Molly smiled in greeting as a tall young woman with long curly hair and a wide smile led the boy over to them. The young woman leaned down.

"Say hello to Daddy's guests, Orlando."

Orlando tightened his grip on his nanny's hand and regarded Molly with suspicion. His mouth remained firmly closed.

"I think that he's rather tired, Sir William. We've had a very exciting day today. Orlando and I had a picnic in the grounds with some of his little friends and then we played games."

Sir William looked affectionately at his son.

"Well, I hope that you won Orlando." He turned to the nanny. "He looks rather tired, Scarlett. Perhaps you had better take him up to his room."

"Very well, Sir William," said Scarlett. "Come along, Orlando."

He watched affectionately as a protesting Orlando was led from the room, and then turned back to Molly.

"Well, I hope that you enjoy your time with us. I must go and greet the other guests."

Molly watched as his tall figure approached a small group by the door. He had, she thought, a certain presence. She removed the umbrella from her drink and studied it for a moment before placing it carefully down on a side table. When she was a child she would have saved it to place in one of the miniature gardens that she was always making. But then, she reflected, liberal as her parents had been, she wouldn't have been drinking cocktails when she was a child. She glanced down at her watch. Jeremy should be back by now. Slightly alarmed when the cats hadn't returned earlier, he had gone out into the grounds to look for them.

"The little sods were up a tree, watching me."

She turned round. Jeremy stood clutching his cocktail. He took a small nervous sip and swallowed it quickly.

"Don't suppose there's any chance of a beer round here?"

Molly laughed.

"I shouldn't think so. Where are the cats now? Are they in?"

Jeremy nodded.

"I had the foresight to take a handful of cat treats with me. I've left the balcony door slightly ajar in case they need to get out again. It should be okay." He paused. "You know Moll, I'm not so sure that bringing them with us was such a great idea. I don't want to spend the whole holiday wondering where they are. Or," he added, "what they're up to."

They both turned as a woman walked confidently through the open French doors. Tall and slim, with unruly grey hair and wild bloodshot eyes, she was clearly the worse for wear. Gathering her wrap around her, she advanced towards them.

"May I introduce myself? I am Lady Pelham."

She extended a thin hand, bare of rings, towards them.

"Oh, I thought…" Molly, flustered, looked towards the small woman who was now standing next to her husband, one small hand on his arm, her head barely up to his shoulder.

"That," said the woman in a loud voice. "Is what is known as a tart."

Behind her stood Carlos, who had finished studying the menu and was now clearly struggling not to laugh. Molly shot him a warning look.

"It's very nice to meet you," said Jeremy giving Molly a 'what do we do now' look. She opened her mouth to speak and then closed it again as, sensing a disturbance behind him, Sir William turned and viewed the scene, his face like thunder. Striding towards them, he gripped the woman's arm and squeezed it hard. He hissed into her face, and pulled her towards him, forcing her to look up.

"Elizabeth, what on earth are you doing here?"

Pulling away from him, the woman stumbled and fell back against a small table. Gathering what shreds of dignity she had left around her, she steadied herself and took a deep breath.

"William. How lovely to see you. Happy birthday, my dear. The children told me that they would be here so I thought that I would make it a proper family reunion."

Sir William looked at her, his expression one of pity mixed with angry frustration.

"You're drunk, Elizabeth. Please leave."

"Oh William, really? I was so looking forward to celebrating your birthday with you. And the tart, of course."

CHAPTER EIGHT

JACOB SAT DOWN in the small Victorian chair and ran his hand along its arms. It was clearly fake, but as fakes go it was pretty good. Bridie and his father must have paid a small fortune to dress Seton Manor to this standard. He stretched his long legs in front of him and looked around. This had been his bedroom when he was a child although it was barely recognisable now. In those days it had contained his narrow single bed, a chest of drawers and a small wardrobe, and the rest of the space had been cluttered with model aeroplanes and toy cars. Now it looked like what it was, an upmarket hotel bedroom decorated with soft muted colours and expensive furnishing. He wondered where his toys were now. Probably gone down to the tip for landfill if Bridie had anything to do with it. They wouldn't have been good enough for Orlando to play with, that was for sure.

He got up and walked over to the tiny fridge tucked discreetly away in the corner of the room. Would he be charged, he wondered, for using the mini bar? It wouldn't surprise him. Well, he'd find out soon enough. He pulled the door open and surveyed the contents. Very nice. Pulling out a small wine bottle he unscrewed the cap and drank straight from the bottle while he reflected on the scene that had taken place earlier downstairs.

Poor mother. She shouldn't have done it but a part of him rather admired her for it. It must have taken courage, albeit clearly of the Dutch sort, to make an entrance like that. That couple she had approached clearly had no idea what to do and had stood embarrassed and uncertain at the prospect of the scene unfolding before them. Funnily enough it had been Bridie who had sorted it out. Tripping over to them in her little tippety-tap high heels she had stood, head on one side, while she surveyed the wreck that their mother had become.

"Poor old dear." She had spoken in that breathy little voice of hers and leaned over his mother who was now sitting in one of the ornate French reproduction chairs, legs stretched out before her and looking defiant. Bridie's cute little lipsticked mouth was pulled down at the corners and her nose wrinkled slightly as though she was staring down at an open drain. She twisted her head and looked up at her husband. "Don't worry, Billy. I'll fetch Guido."

And Guido had arrived. The general handyman, driver and sorter out of all annoying problems, which included removing the former Lady Pelham from Seton Manor. He'd done it well, Jacob had to admit. Grasping her under one elbow he had gently but firmly raised her from the chair and propelled her from the room, giving her no time to protest. Outside they had heard an engine start. Presumably Guido had driven her home, given that she could barely stand up. He wondered suddenly how his mother had got there. Her cottage wasn't far away, easily within walking distance, but perhaps she had driven. Surely not in that state? He wouldn't put it past her. She had become increasingly reckless of late. He'd go out and check later if her car was there. If so then presumably Guido could run it back in the morning.

Not for the first time he found himself wondering about Guido. Nobody was really called Guido. Were they? At least not when they had a distinct estuary accent. A broad man of medium height, interesting looking rather than handsome, with a craggy face and intensely blue eyes, he was probably in his mid-thirties. Where he had come from, Jacob had no idea. Guido had seemed to arrive out of nowhere. He never spoke unless spoken to and gave nothing of himself away. But wherever he had come from, he was well-established at the Manor. Living in the apartment above the garages, he pretty much kept himself to himself and did whatever he was asked to do. Nothing seemed to faze him. Not even, it appeared, removing elderly drunken ladies from the premises.

He glanced down at his watch. It was nearly time for dinner and one of the many things that his father would not tolerate was lateness. He got up reluctantly and then sat down again. He still had twenty minutes. He took another swig from the little wine bottle and let his mind drift back to the conversation earlier with Edward and Emily. He wasn't surprised at their tales of woe, not really. Edward had been a fool to marry Delia in the first place and he had told him so, not that Edward had thanked him for it. He didn't have anything against Delia personally but she got through money like there was no tomorrow. As a teenager she had flitted around London with her society friends, always in the best restaurants and clubs and always dressed in the height of fashion, and she had clearly seen no reason to change when she married.

Would she, he wondered, leave Edward when she found out what he had been up to? He suspected that she might. He really couldn't see her getting a job to make ends meet. Now he thought about it, he doubted that she'd ever worked at all apart from some brief spells at a friend's fashion house when she felt like it. Try as Edward might to explain the situation to her, Jacob suspected that Delia would be completely uncomprehending. It would never occur to her that she might pick up the reins. After some initial bewilderment she would simply drift back to her rich parents and take the twins with her.

Poor Ed. He might have himself to blame for the mess that he'd got himself into but he was still his little brother. Anyway, as someone had once said, everything that happens to us is our fault, but that's not our fault. And as for Emily... he sighed. Emily was clever in many respects, she was bright and attractive and she had a great capacity for making friends, but she had no more business sense than the birds in the trees. He was surprised that their father had ever backed her. Although that of course was before Bridie had come on the scene. And, unlike his sons whom he expected to succeed at everything, even a game of Ludo, their father hadn't really expected anything much of Emily at all. He pretty much regarded her craft and book shop as a hobby, something to occupy her until she got married. Not that any wedding bells seemed likely to ring in the near, or even the distant, future. Every relationship Emily had ever had ended badly. The last one had been a spectacular disaster.

Eight years younger than Emily and calling himself a poet, Tristan had moved into her smart little house and made himself completely at home. As far as Jacob could see, he had apparently felt no need to contribute anything, other than his genius of course, and had lived very comfortably until he moved out when he met somebody else. After first helping himself to five hundred pounds from Emily's bank account. But who was he to judge either Emily or Edward? He had problems of his own and they weren't the sort to go away of their own accord.

He felt his forehead crinkle with anxiety. Why, he wondered, hadn't he confided in his brother and sister when they had been talking earlier? It would have been so easy to do, especially when they had both been so honest, and it wasn't as though he didn't trust them. But somehow the words just wouldn't come. He rubbed his hand across his eyes. As the oldest child and the first born son, a huge amount had been not so much expected as demanded of him. And he had, for the most part, met those demands. While he had resisted the pressure to join his father's business, knowing full well that he was temperamentally unsuited to such a life, he had come up to scratch in other areas. He had played cricket for the school, he had gained a place at a good university, he had married the daughter of a prosperous farmer and star of the local tennis club, and he had worked his way up in the Civil Service and held what was, by anybody's standards, a pretty senior position. Until the letter had arrived.

At least it had been a letter and not an email, he had been spared that. He could still recall the terrifying sense of shock. For the first time he had understood what breaking out in a cold sweat really meant. The word redundancy had leaped off the page and smacked him straight in the eyes so that he could barely breathe. Some bastard cabinet minister had decided that his department was no longer required. Following an internal review, three departments were scheduled to be scrapped, his being one of them. It was what the pompous little twat had described as otiose. The letter had been postmarked on a Friday, and it being a bank holiday, he had three whole days to stew on it. Three whole days to go about trying to pretend to be normal while his world tilted on its axis. He had known, of course, that the internal review was under way but it had never, not in the proverbial million years, occurred to him that his own department was at risk. In between frantically trying to work out what his redundancy payment might be, he had reassured himself that there was no shame in it. It happened to people all the time. But who was he kidding? It didn't happen to people like him.

On the Tuesday he had demanded a meeting with the minister, claiming that his seniority entitled him to at least that. He had sat opposite the man, despising his snouty little face and sticking out ears, and listened as the words etched themselves painfully in his memory. Each department, the minister had explained slowly and patiently as if talking to somebody who was mentally defective, must be fit for purpose. The problem being, he had continued, that it was no longer entirely clear, in Jacob's case, what that purpose was. He had smiled as he said it, a sad little smile as though assuring Jacob that he felt his pain. Jacob had stared at him, feeling the words bounce against his brain and noting the minister's surreptitious glance at his watch and the slight shuffling of papers on his desk. Jacob recognised the signals. They were ones he had used himself often enough.

He knew about this minister. They all did. There wasn't much that went on in the corridors of power that even the lowliest civil servant didn't know about. And this bloke was ambitious. He fancied himself as the next PM and word had it that he was already sharpening the knives and touting for support. Jacob was almost tempted to laugh. Didn't the man know that he who wields the sword rarely wears the crown? But, be that as it may, the sword was currently pointing directly at him and there was nothing that he could do about it. Instead of squaring his shoulders and making the case against his fate as he had determined that he would, he had simply sat there paralysed, like a lamb to the slaughter, afraid of making a fuss, fearful of appearing less than a gentleman. Because, after all, he had his pride. And he would need good references.

Felicity had met the news in silence. It had been almost two years since they had shared a bed, let alone seen any action in one and her indifference to almost everything that he said or did had become the norm. To all intents and purposes they were living separate lives. He had wondered sometimes if the children noticed and had decided eventually that they didn't. They were both at an age where their own interests were paramount and their parents were largely irrelevant, other than as a useful resource when it came to money or lifts home from parties. Eventually Felicity had said,

"What will you do?"

Not, he noted, what will we do. But at least Felicity, as an administrator with a local design company, had a job. The problem was that it was only part-time and it didn't pay particularly well. In fact, it really only covered what his mother used to call pin money, whatever that was, but it was something. They probably could, in the very short term, keep the ship afloat at least as far as essentials went. But for how long, he had no idea. The gym membership and one of the cars would have to go, along with the cleaner and their planned trip to the states later in the year. Luckily both his son and daughter attended the nearby state secondary so there were no school fees to pay but presumably there would be university fees to meet in the future. His redundancy payment would be the minimum that the Civil Service could get away with but, looking on the positive side, it should still be a reasonable sum. After all, he had worked there since leaving university. And that, he reflected bitterly, was a part of the problem. Every job that he had applied for had come to nothing. He had been invited to only one interview and hadn't even made it to the second round. The truth was that nobody wanted an over-educated man, with only a narrow and specific range of skills, in his forties.

Perhaps he would tell Emily and Edward after all. It would be a relief to be able to talk about it and he knew that they would be on his side. They might annoy each other from time to time, but when the chips were down they always stuck together. He smiled suddenly, remembering the time when he and Ed had been throwing a cricket ball about in the grounds and had stared in panic-stricken horror as it went straight through an open window and broke a lamp in their father's study. Emily had told their father that she had done it. They all knew that she would get away with it, especially if she pretended to cry. And got away with it she had. Their father had simply smiled indulgently and told her that she should be more careful.

He pulled his mobile from his pocket and called up Emily's number.

CHAPTER NINE

AUBREY LOOKED AROUND nervously. Above him the early morning sun sparkled down on the blue of the water. It had seemed like a lark to jump on the floating thing but now it had drifted out towards the middle of the pool and he had no idea how to get back to the edge again. He'd heard somebody once say that as tigers could swim that obviously meant that all cats could swim but he had no intention of testing the theory out right now, especially as the person who had said it was one of the more intellectually challenged screws at Sunny Bank rescue centre. He peered anxiously down at the water and wondered how deep it was. He must be getting soft. There was a time when he would never have done such a foolish thing. And where was Vincent? He had been here a few seconds ago. He lifted his head as a rustling sound came from the nearby shrubbery.

"Use your paws," hissed Vincent.

"What?"

"Use your paws," he repeated. And raising his own paws he made a paddling movement.

Aubrey nodded and, shifting over on to his stomach, began to paddle his way towards the little steps by the side of the pool. It was harder work than it looked. He turned his head at the sound of voices. Vincent moved closer towards the edge of the pool.

"Faster."

Obediently, Aubrey moved as fast as his paws would take him and reached the edge just as two people came into view. Scrambling up the steps, water dripping from his fur, he ran with Vincent towards the loungers and flopped down beneath one. A small auburn haired woman sank down on the one next to it and dropped her head in her hands. The folds of her pink lace dressing gown fell away and revealed a pair of flimsy pyjamas with small pink hearts printed across them.

"Oh Billy, what are we going to do?"

The tall man in his silk paisley dressing gown, crouched down in front of her and took her hands.

"Now don't get in a panic, Bridie. I expect that he's just gone off exploring. He's probably playing somewhere."

The woman lifted her head and stared woefully at him.

"He's never done it before. What if somebody's taken him? What if he's stuck somewhere or injured himself?" She stood up suddenly. "I'm going to start looking right now."

The man tugged at her dressing gown and pulled her back down.

"Don't overreact, my dear. You must stay calm. Let's just go through it again, we may have missed something. Now, start at the beginning."

The woman reached into her dressing gown pocket and then dabbed at her eyes with a small lace-edged handkerchief.

"Well, I was doing my hair." She sniffed and swallowed. "When nanny came in and said that Orlando wasn't in his bed. And I said, what do you mean, he's not in his bed. And she said, he's not in his bed."

Aubrey and Vincent looked at each other.

"I think she's trying to say that he's not in his bed," said Vincent.

Aubrey laughed.

The man nodded patiently.

"And what did you do then?"

"Well, I went to the nursery. And he wasn't in his bed. It had been slept in but he wasn't in it. And that's when I called you. Oh Billy, what if something's happened to him?"

The man covered her small hand with his own.

"Don't worry, my dear. We will get dressed and search the grounds and the manor. My bet is that he's just hiding somewhere."

IN THE DRAWING room Emily, Jacob and Edward sat quietly, not speaking. In the hall the big grandfather clock struck ten, the ponderous chime echoing through the house. From upstairs they could hear their step-mother wailing and shouting, the words indistinct. The three siblings strained their ears to hear their father's voice above the noise, trying to catch the low deep tones attempting to soothe. Emily fidgeted slightly and turned to Jacob.

"Poor Daddy, it sounds like he's having a hard time of it. Do you think that we should go up and help?"

Jacob shook his head.

"No, I don't think so. I suspect that the sight of us three will only make Bridie worse. Father will know what to do." He sighed. "Father always knows what to do."

After waking his three older children and informing them of the situation, Sir William had indeed taken control of the situation. He had organised a thorough search in which Guido had volunteered to search the grounds with Bridie, while he Emily, Edward and Jacob had searched the house. Edward had even climbed up into the attics and emerged, cobwebs clinging to his clothes, and shaking his head. Watching the proceedings with considerable interest were Aubrey and Vincent. Something was obviously up. What they wanted to know was, what that something was.

The indoor searchers had regrouped in the drawing room, each of them subdued. Bridie re-joined them having, Emily noticed, managed to quell her terror sufficiently to apply some make-up, although not the usual full face. She had contented herself with just a flick of mascara and a slick of pale lipstick. Did she, Emily wondered, ever present a bare face to the world? She had watched as Bridie sat silently on one of the small sofas, picking at the knee of her blue cut-off jeans with a small manicured nail, one tanned leg tucked beneath her. All their faces were turned to Sir William. Eventually he had spoken.

"I think that we must call the police. Don't panic, my dear." He turned to Bridie who started upwards in protest, and stroked the top of her head. "I'm still sure that he's just hiding somewhere, playing a little joke on us. But the police are equipped to deal with these situations. They have search dogs and so on. They'll soon find the little rascal."

He had pulled his mobile from his pocket just as it began to vibrate. The brevity of the text had been shocking. Sir William had read it in silence before holding it up for the group to see. We have the child. Say nothing. Do not call the police. Wait for further instructions. Bridie had rushed upstairs, followed immediately by Sir William.

The noise from upstairs ceased and the drawing room door opened. Their father, pale but resolute, strode into the room. Jacob stared at him. He realised, for the first time, that his father never just walked anywhere. He always strode. Perhaps that was one of the secrets of his success. He ought to try it himself sometime, Felicity might have a bit more respect for him. Emily jumped up to greet her father.

"Oh, Daddy. What's happening?"

"I have decided that for the time being we must do nothing. Therefore we must do as we have been asked and wait for further instructions. Bridie is beside herself and I have given her a large brandy to calm her down."

His three older children stared at him as he helped himself to whisky from the decanter. He turned and faced them, his expression stern.

"You will, none of you, say a word about this, not even to the staff." He took a large gulp of whisky. "To all outward appearances everything must carry on as normal. We must not say or do anything that could put Orlando at risk. Also, there are guests in the hotel and in the apartments, some of them have brought children with them. If this gets out it will be ruinous for the business."

Edward choked back a desire to laugh. His father's youngest son was missing, almost certainly abducted, and he was concerned about the effect on the business. He stood up.

"I'm going for a walk."

CHAPTER TEN

OUT IN THE grounds Edward felt the heat of the day beginning to rise. By noon it would probably be unbearable. Bending down, he tugged off his shoes and socks and sank his bare feet into the lawn, curling his toes beneath them. It was oddly soothing. He walked on a little further, feeling the comforting springiness of the turf beneath his feet. It was something that he had liked to do as a child and a habit for which his mother had often scolded him, warning of cut toes and colds in the head. Given that their father was always working, their mother had more or less taken sole responsibility for them. It had always been she who had been ready to stick plasters on cut knees or to comfort them when their pet hamster had died, assuring them that Hammy had gone to hamster heaven where there was an endless supply of strawberries and lots of hamster friends to play with. And they had believed her and organised an elaborate hamster funeral, complete with Emily playing All Through The Night on her recorder.

How different their childhood had been from Orlando's. There had been no nannies for them, not like Bridie and Father had for Orlando, not that many of them seemed to stay for very long. One of them had lasted for less than a week. He couldn't say that he blamed her. He thought about his little half-brother and his disconcerting habit of staring at people. The truth was that none of them liked him. He was a difficult child to like. It didn't help that every time he opened his mouth to speak Bridie insisted that everybody should stop whatever they were doing and listen and wonder at the pearls of wisdom that dropped from his podgy little mouth. Sturdy, bordering on the overweight, it seemed that Orlando's every whim was catered to. Nothing was too good for him. His clothes carried designer labels and his toys came from Harrods. His last birthday party, his fifth, had been fairground themed.

Held in the grounds of Seton Manor the party had been captured on video by Bridie and had featured a real merry go round, a clown and magic show for entertainment, and catering provided by a private chef. The guests were carefully selected children from good families and had been requested to dress as pirates. And dress as pirates they did. On being forced to watch the video by Bridie and his father, Edward had concluded that most of the pirate outfits had been professionally made. There was no suggestion of a last minute dive into the dressing up box. And naturally, all the children came bearing expensive gifts. Not like their own birthday parties, he reflected. Their guests had been the children from the village and involved home-made jelly and blancmange, jam sandwiches and pass the parcel. And none the worse for it.

The arrival of Orlando had been something that none of them had anticipated. It had been enough of a shock that their father had remarried, but that he might father another son in his seventies was something that they had never considered. Although, when they had talked about it afterwards they all agreed that they should have seen it coming. Of course Bridie was going to secure her position. And what better way to do it? But much as they disliked Orlando, they liked Bridie even less although none of them dared to show it. He sighed. Bridie was the only weakness that any of them had ever seen their father exhibit but, like everything else in his life, he didn't muck around.

When he wanted something he went all out to get it and woe betide anybody that got in his way.

What had Bridie done that was so special, he wondered, to get his father to disrupt his whole life? Up until then he had seemed reasonably content with the way things were. His business had gone from strength to strength and it hadn't been too long before he had made his first million. While his relationship with his wife hadn't been what might be described as passionate, especially as they grew older, he had seemed satisfied enough. He had his club and his golf, his business interests, his occasional flings. Their mother had been happy enough at home when they were children. She had never indicated, at least openly, that she would like to do anything else. As far as Edward could recall, she had enjoyed her needlepoint and baking, her sherry before dinner and her lunches with friends. It was true that she occasionally, well, often, drank too much once they had all left home but Edward couldn't say that he blamed her. She was probably bored.

His parents had, he reflected, been what might be termed a traditional married couple. Slightly old-fashioned perhaps but not completely untypical of their generation. Perhaps Bridie had brought their father a sense of excitement, the thrill of the new. Perhaps she hadn't been the push over that they had all thought. Perhaps, unlike her predecessors, she had played hard to get. Maybe she had led him a bit of a dance and he had discovered that he liked it. It was probably exactly that trait that made him such a good man of business. For Edward, it was exactly the sort of feeling that he didn't like. He liked certainty and familiarity, it made him feel secure. He liked looking in his diary and knowing exactly what would happen that day. It was just those characteristics that had made him such a good solicitor. Until he had started helping himself to client funds, that is. The only unpredictable thing he had ever done was to marry Delia.

He had met Delia at a party. It wasn't the sort of party that he was usually invited to. In fact he couldn't remember now how the invitation had come about. At the time he had been going out with another girl, the daughter of a friend of his mother's whom he had met at the local youth club when they were teenagers, but she had been out of town that evening and he had been at a loose end. The girl had been called Katy, a wispily pretty girl that he had assumed, without too much enthusiasm, that he would eventually marry. They had even gone so far as to talk about possible venues for an engagement party. And then Delia had happened. Delia had struck him like a whirlwind. With her party life and society friends, he had been completely dazzled by her. He had pursued her with a stubborn obstinacy and determination that surprised even himself. Perhaps, he thought, he was more like his father than he had realised.

He sighed and pulled his socks and shoes back on. What he wanted to do right now was go home, even though the house was empty. No, what he really wanted to do was turn the clock back ten months before all his troubles started.

CHAPTER ELEVEN

EMILY STARED AT her reflection in the bathroom mirror. The youngest of the three siblings, on days like this she looked like the eldest. Her fair skin that she had inherited from her mother didn't do well in the heat and her eyes looked baggy and tired. She swept her hair up with one hand and secured it with a clip. She had once heard the style described as an instant face lift. She let the clip go again. If anything, it made her look worse. No wonder Tristan had left her. On days like today she looked old enough to be his mother.

Tristan. He had been such fun to start with. If anybody could have been described as living in the moment, it was him. She had met him at a music festival that she had been persuaded to go to by her friends and he had been holding court in one of the beer tents. He had noticed her straight away and she been flattered by his interest in her, and charmed by his loud noisy friends, all of whom seemed to be involved in some kind of artistic endeavour. It was only later she noticed that he rarely put his hand in his pocket even though they went out most evenings to various bars and clubs. He had always assumed that she would pick up the bill and, like a fool, she had done.

If she was honest with herself she had sometimes wondered if he had known who she was before he spoke to her, if he had been aware that she was the daughter of a multi-millionaire. Whatever the truth of it, there had come a point at which she had started to get a little tired of it all. There were evenings when she wanted to come home and put her feet up in front of the television. Sit watching an old movie with a glass of wine and maybe eat a jacket potato from a tray on her lap. But she had gone along with it all, afraid of doing anything that might draw attention to the differences between them, afraid that he would get bored with her.

She had known as soon as she had arrived home that last night that the house was empty. The very air seemed still. He hadn't even bothered to find a decent piece of paper. Scribbled on the back of a used envelope he had simply said that he needed more space. How much more space, she had wondered, had he needed? She was in the shop all day or out on buying trips, leaving him in peace to write his poems in her spare room which he had turned into a study. It wasn't like there were ever any demands made on him. When it came to domestic duties, he never seemed to feel obliged to do anything around the house, not even unload the dishwasher, and it certainly never seemed to occur to him to do any shopping. He'd rather go without than walk the hundred yards to the corner shop to buy milk, although he'd complain about the fridge being empty when she got home.

In her heart, apart from her wounded pride, she knew that she what she really felt when he left was a sense of relief. Apart from anything else, she couldn't have imagined introducing him to Daddy. The only member of the family who had met him had been Jacob, who, taking his older brother duties seriously, had given her a stern lecture on what he called wasting herself. Well, he hadn't been wrong. Once Tristan had realised that she didn't have unlimited access to her father's millions he had tripped off to pastures new. The last she had heard, he was living with a widow in Eastbourne.

She glanced down at her watch. It was later than she'd thought. She'd have to go back down again soon, if only to find out what was happening. Her mind ran back over the scene at the dinner table the previous evening. Following the impromptu meeting in Jacob's room and the shock of his revelations, they had trailed down to dinner in sombre mood ready to celebrate her father's birthday. Orlando, bulging out of his sailor suit like a badly stuffed sausage, had sat at his mother's side, his piggy little eyes surveying the huge ostentatious birthday cake which stood in the centre of the table and which had been created by a prestigious bakery in London. His father, still furious at the embarrassment caused to him by his former wife, had been taciturn and uncommunicative. Emily, Jacob and Edward had made polite conversation while they waited for the moment when Bridie would announce that she must put her little sweetheart to bed. Putting her little sweetheart to bed was something that Bridie did herself every night. Everything else was left to nanny.

As Bridie had left the room, pulling her reluctant little sweetheart behind her, his face smeared with cake, Emily had cleared her throat. They had all voted earlier that she should do the talking, given that she was their father's favourite. In so far as he had one. They all suspected that in his heart he despised all three of them for not being the success that he was. Jacob should have followed him into the business, Edward should have been a High Court judge at the very least, and Emily should have married a peer of the realm and graced the pages of Country Life. Their father was nothing if not traditional, at least when it came to his children.

Emily swallowed nervously and began.

"Father, we were rather wondering, that is, Jacob, Edward and I…"

Her father had cut across her, raising the palm of his hand to emphasise his words.

"If it's money, Emily, then I'm afraid that the answer is no. You have, all three of you, had more than a good start. You must stand on your own two feet now. I have invested considerable sums in the development of Seton Manor and I really cannot spare anymore."

Emily had felt the hatred rise. She didn't see Bridie standing on her own two feet. Their father was a millionaire several times over, he could easily afford to help them out. The sums that each of them needed to dig themselves out of their respective holes were mere drops in the ocean. If he gave them half of what he and Bridie spent on that little shit Orlando it would go a long way towards solving their problems. The nanny's wages alone would pay off most of her debts from the shop. She had subsided into silence, uncertain what to say next, and shortly afterwards Sir William had left the room, claiming that he must say goodnight to his youngest son. Edward's shoulders had slumped and he had taken a huge draught from his wine glass.

"He's obviously not going to help us out and we haven't even told him yet what the problems are."

Emily had reached across the table towards him and patted his hand.

"Don't panic, Ed. There'll be a way."

Her eyes met Jacob's.

CHAPTER TWELVE

DOWNSTAIRS JACOB AND Edward sat at the table in the small morning room. The hotel guests were served in the formal dining room and they could hear the rattle and clatter of cutlery and glass as the staff made the room ready for lunch. Through the open window a faint summer breeze drifted into the room, bringing with it a billowing scent of summer. They looked up as Emily came in and sat down.

"All right, Em?" asked Edward.

Emily nodded.

"I wonder if Daddy and Bridie will be down for lunch?"

As she spoke the door opened again and her father and stepmother entered the room. Bridie stared at them in sullen silence, the dark shadows under her eyes clearly evident as their father pulled a chair back for her. He cleared his throat.

"We have received another text. The people who are holding Orlando want two million pounds in order for his safe return."

"Are you going to pay it?" asked Jacob.

"Don't be ridiculous Jacob," Bridie snapped. "Of course we are."

Jacob narrowed his eyes. You mean Father is, he thought. I doubt if you've got twenty quid to your name, let alone two million.

Sir William ignored the interruption and continued speaking.

"The kidnappers have indicated that they will give us further instructions as to where to pay the money in due course. We have been requested not to call the police and I think that for the time being we must accede to that request."

Edward met Emily's eye across the table and raised one eyebrow. It wasn't a request, it was an order. But, of course, their father never took orders from anybody. Emily looked down and began drawing patterns on the table cloth with her finger.

"Who do you think is responsible?" she asked, without looking up.

Sir William looked thoughtful

"I have considered that. So far, I have not been able to come up with an answer. If we could trace the phone from which the messages have been sent it would help. But I expect he or she has used a burner phone."

Edward stared at his father. A burner phone? Burner phones were cheap throw away kit, bought for cash and used by criminals. How on earth did his father know about things like that? But then, he reflected, of course he did. Knowing about such things was part of what had made him such a successful business man.

"I have, of course," continued Sir William, "sacked nanny. She will be gone by the end of the day. Orlando is her responsibility and she has signally failed in that duty."

"I never did like that girl," said Bridie. "She had ideas above her station."

Emily bit her lip. That's a joke, she thought, coming from you. Anyway, Orlando is your responsibility. Yours and Daddy's, not Scarlett's. Poor Scarlett. A young friendly woman, Scarlett had surely done her best with what was, by anybody's standards, a difficult child. But, to Emily's bemusement, Scarlett had seemed genuinely fond of Orlando. She certainly hadn't seemed to mind taking him out and playing endless games with him, which she always allowed him to win. Where she had come from she wasn't sure, but she had certainly lasted longer than any of the other nannies. What was Scarlett supposed to have done anyway? Sat up all night and watched over the child? Suddenly Bridie banged the table with her small fist, making her rings rattle. She glared at the three siblings, her eyes narrowed.

"It's your mother that's behind this. I know it is."

"What do you mean?" Jacob leaned forward, his usually pale face flushed red. "What do you mean, it's our mother?"

Bridie stared defiantly back at him.

"It's obvious. She hates me. She hates us. She's never got over Billy leaving her. This is her way of getting her revenge." She threw her head back and laughed suddenly, a shrill unpleasant noise that held no mirth. "If she'd been any sort of wife, Billy would never have left her in the first place. God, who'd want to wake up to that old bag in the mornings?"

Jacob gripped the edge of the table. Better than waking up to you, you over-painted little slut, he thought. Father was a fool to have ever gone anywhere near you. Bridie leaned back in her chair and eyed the three siblings, her expression one of contempt.

"She's just an ugly, nasty old drunk who can't stand to see other people happy. She was here last night, we all saw her, making a scene. I think, Billy," she said, turning to her husband, "that we should get over there and search her house."

"Father," Emily began. "Surely…"

Sir William put his arm around his wife and drew her close to him.

"Bridie may have a point, Emily. Elizabeth has made no attempt at all to reconcile herself to the fact of our divorce and my remarriage. And she has certainly never given any indication of having any affection for Orlando."

"Why should she?" Edward glared at his father. "Why on earth should she?"

"Because, Edward," replied Sir William. "That would be the civilised thing to do. She has shown a sad lack of dignity throughout and has become, I am afraid, a very bitter and angry woman."

Edward shook his head in despair. Sometimes his father was truly unbelievable.

"How she might have entered the house," Sir William continued. "I have no idea. But of all people she has, you must agree, a very detailed knowledge of Seton Manor. Although, I must admit, I cannot think how she could have persuaded Orlando to go away with her."

Try a giant size bar of chocolate, thought Jacob. Throw a dozen bags of crisps in his direction. He suddenly had the ludicrous image of somebody letting down a fishing line before Orlando's window, on the end of which was suspended a big bag of chocolate with which to tempt him out. He tightened his mouth. Now would seriously not be a good time to start laughing. The way he felt at the moment, he knew that if he started he wouldn't be able to stop. And if he started, it would start Emily and Edward off too. It was something that they had suffered from since they were children and indeed on one occasion they had been marched out of Sunday school, collapsing in uncontrollable laughter, after Edward had spotted that the Sunday school's teacher had her dress caught in her knickers, revealing a rather large dimpled backside.

"But frankly," said Sir William, unaware of his eldest's son struggle to contain himself, "I sometimes feel that I am at my wits end. I have done everything that I can to provide for her, we all know that she is not in the best of health, but she has become a very difficult person." He drew his hand across his forehead in the manner of a world weary man who has done nothing but his very best, yet feels misjudged. "I think sometimes that I hardly knew her."

Emily swallowed hard and pressed her lips together. He was actually serious. He meant it. True, he had provided for their mother in terms of giving her a home but she didn't actually own it. She was a tenant. His tenant, and as such she was subject to notice whenever it suited him. She might be his ex-wife but as far as he was concerned she was still his property and he called the shots. It was also true that he had allowed her a basic income but surely that was the least she could have expected given the length of their marriage and the size of his wealth, particularly as she was past the age when she might have been expected to go out and get a job. And as for saying that he felt that he had hardly known her, it was just ridiculous. Their mother had been nothing but a loyal and devoted wife throughout their long marriage and had always had his best interests at heart. She had supported him in everything that he did and she should now be enjoying her later years in the family home. Instead of which she was stuck in that damp little cottage on the edge of the estate where she couldn't even get a decent phone signal.

It was all down to bloody Bridie. From the moment that she had arrived on the scene, Bridie had swung through their lives like a miniature wrecking ball, destroying everything that they held dear. Their mother's world and, to a lesser extent, their own, had completely collapsed under the weight of her father's infatuation. Everything that they had known had been swept away and they had been left confused and uncertain, hardly able to grasp what was happening. And it had all happened so quickly. It seemed sometimes to Emily that one moment she was driving up for a lovely family visit with her parents and the next there was this nasty little bitch pervading the house and busying herself obliterating all the happy memories. Not content with that, she never missed an opportunity to belittle and insult her predecessor. Had Bridie really managed to poison their father's mind so much that he believed what he was saying? Anyway, if it was true that their mother had become embittered, was it any wonder? It had been humiliating enough to be deserted, but to be deserted for somebody like Bridie...

"Look at your mother," said Bridie, leaning forward and pinning her elbows on the table, the venom dripping from her mean little mouth. "Just look at her, at the state of her. She's got no self-respect. She looks like some sort of bag lady. The drunken raddled old bitch. All that grey hair hanging down. Why doesn't she get herself a proper hair cut?"

Edward leaned across the table, his face white.

"Perhaps she would if she had a decent amount to live on. If father had provided properly for her, as he should have done. But you, you fucking tart, you've taken everything away from her. Away from us. Do you think everybody can't see what a money-grubbing little whore you are?"

Sir William rose to his feet, his face scarlet.

"Edward," he thundered, "you will apologise to your stepmother immediately."

Kicking back his chair like a recalcitrant teenager, Edward rose and left the room.

CHAPTER THIRTEEN

SITTING PEACEFULLY ON the window ledge, basking in the sun, and casually eavesdropping on the scene in the morning room through the open window, Aubrey and Vincent looked at each other.

"Looks like that kid hasn't turned up," said Aubrey. "Can't say I'll miss him."

And nor would he. Catching him peacefully asleep under an oak tree the previous day, Orlando had sneaked up behind him and pulled his tail. Not just pulled it but given it a sharp yank that had been really painful, and then he had run away laughing as fast as his chubby little legs would take him. Aubrey had been shocked, as well as in pain. Most of his experience with children had been positive. Any pain or discomfort that had ever been caused was usually a result of over-enthusiastic hugging or stroking. But this attack by Orlando had been completely deliberate and had caught him unawares.

Vincent nodded and looked thoughtful. In the early hours of this morning, awake early and keen to explore, they had both seen a shadowy hooded figure standing outside Seton Manor. Impossible to tell whether it was a man or a woman, it had stood for a moment looking up at the windows as if it was waiting for something. Sure enough, a tiny light flicked on and then off. The figure had nodded to itself and crept stealthily away. At the time they had thought little of it, humans did all sorts of strange things. But now he thought about it, it did seem a bit odd. Why would anybody be creeping about at that time of the morning? And the figure definitely hadn't wanted to be seen.

Aubrey jumped down from the window ledge and shook himself.

"I expect the kid will turn up," he said. "He's probably got locked in somewhere or something." Getting locked in was a common occurrence in the cat world, and one that they generally had learned to avoid. Tales of cats being locked in garages and sheds and then slowly starving to death were rife in the feline world and the moment any of their number went missing there would usually be a search party out. "I mean, who would want him anyway?"

"Money," said Vincent.

Aubrey stared at him, his mouth open.

"What? You mean he's worth something?"

"To some people."

Aubrey closed his mouth again. People would never cease to amaze him. He would have thought it more likely that people would pay to keep Orlando away. Ah well. It was nothing to him. Anyway, he was getting hungry. It must be about time for a little something.

IN THE POOL, Jeremy was attempting his fifth length, using a style which seemed to involve a lot of splashing and occasional clutching at the side to catch his breath. Molly and Carlos watched him affectionately.

"He'll be ready for the Olympics at that rate," said Carlos.

Molly laughed and leaned back on the lounger, one hand shielding her eyes from the sun.

"It's good to see him enjoying himself. I don't think that he's checked his email once since we've been here." She glanced down at her watch. "What time are you expecting Teddy?"

"In about an hour. Her dad's dropping her off. Hello Aubrey." He dropped his hand down and stroked Aubrey's head. "Casper's coming too. Teddy's dad knows Sir William and he's said that they can camp for a few nights in the little copse."

He spoke the last word with a slightly self-conscious air. When Teddy had messaged him about the camping he had needed to look the word copse up.

"Well, I hope that Casper will behave himself." Molly sounded doubtful as she spoke. Aubrey grinned. He very much hoped that Casper would not behave himself. "What will they do about showers and so on? They're welcome to use our bathroom if they want to."

"I'll tell them but Sir William has said that they can use the hotel. Teddy said that Sir William told her dad that he was thinking of introducing glamping." He paused. "Do you think he meant camping?"

Molly smiled.

"No, I think he meant glamping."

CHAPTER FOURTEEN

CARLOS LOOKED AROUND him in the gathering dusk and took a great lungful of clean air. Maybe there was something to this countryside stuff after all. Next to him Teddy picked up the sleeping bags that she had laid to air on the grass and shook them. He smiled down at her. He couldn't remember the last time he had felt so happy. After Teddy and Casper had arrived they had left their father drinking coffee with Molly and Jeremy and the three of them had headed off to the copse to set up camp. They had found the perfect spot. A small glade, surrounded by trees, it had offered both shelter and light. Carlos had been secretly dreading putting up the tents, memories of a fishing weekend with Jeremy and struggling with big clanging tent poles being at the forefront of his mind. It wasn't so much that he minded struggling with the tent poles, what he minded was being found wanting in front of Teddy. He needn't have worried. Teddy and Casper had brought with them small tents of the pop-up variety, one each to sleep in and one to store their stuff.

"I'd better be getting back soon. Molly's cooking dinner. Are you sure that you don't want to come? She said to ask you."

Teddy shook her head.

"No, we'll be fine. Mum packed us loads of sandwiches and some cake and crisps and stuff. If Casper hasn't eaten them all yet." She glanced across at her younger brother as she spoke, who was busy gathering sticks and tying them together. "Casper, if that's for a fire, forget it. Dad told us that Sir William has strictly forbidden any type of camp fire."

Casper pulled a face and dropped the bundle of sticks.

"Only a small one," he protested.

"Casper," Teddy spoke patiently. "Not even a small one. Our neighbours still haven't forgiven Mum and Dad for you setting fire to their shed."

"I didn't do it on purpose. I was making fireworks."

"Well, you shouldn't have been. Anyway, why didn't you do it in our own shed?"

"Theirs is bigger. Was bigger," he corrected himself.

Carlos grinned. It felt really good to be back with the two of them. Teddy turned to Carlos.

"Can you come back later? After dinner?"

Carlos nodded. He had half-thought of asking Molly and Jeremy if he could stay with Teddy and Casper in the copse but had then changed his mind. They had booked a two room apartment for a holiday for the three of them and it didn't seem fair to spend half of it with other people, even if was Teddy and Casper. Anyway, he had promised Molly that he would take responsibility for the cats.

MOLLY OPENED THE oven and looked at the fish pie that she had brought from home. Almost done. Perhaps tomorrow they could all eat in the hotel restaurant, Teddy and Casper too, if they wanted to. She looked up as Jeremy came in.

"Did Jonathan get off all right?"

Jeremy nodded.

"Yes. Nice bloke, had an interesting chat."

After drinking coffee with Molly, Teddy's father and Jeremy had wandered over to the hotel bar and spent a pleasant hour in the late afternoon sunshine drinking lager on the terrace.

"He's quite worried about Casper, though," Jeremy continued.

Molly raised her eyebrows.

"I'm not surprised. How many schools has he been expelled from now?"

"Three. The last time was for introducing something that he called rat racing."

"Rat racing?" Molly looked puzzled.

"Racing rats. Real ones. He persuaded a group of boys to bring a rat each into school and then opened a book on them before racing them. In a classroom. During a history lesson. He told the headmaster that he was raising money for the National Rat Federation to re-home destitute rats."

Molly laughed.

"Did the headmaster believe him?"

"Not for a second."

"What happened to the rats?"

"Probably still running around the school somewhere. I expect that they've been entered for their GCSE's by now. Anyway, the headmaster told Jonathan that while he admired Casper's ingenuity and creativity, he was concerned about the adverse effect that he appeared to have on the other boys. Bear in mind that Casper was already on a last chance for planting cannabis in the school garden. He said that he thought they were tomato plants and his plan was to feed the world's starving poor."

"On tomatoes?"

"Apparently."

Jeremy reached across and poured himself a glass of wine from the open bottle on the kitchen work top.

"You know, Moll, there seemed a funny atmosphere up at the hotel this afternoon. I mean, when we went to Sir William's birthday drinks, everybody was quite jolly. Well, apart from the scene when the first Lady Pelham made her grand entrance. But this afternoon it was different. I don't know, it's difficult to put my finger on it, but it was like everybody was holding their breath. Sir William's older children were out on the terrace too. They sort of had their heads together but they all stopped talking when we sat down. Then Lady Pelham came out with a drink in her hand, took one look at them and marched straight back indoors."

"Perhaps she just thought that it was too hot out there?" suggested Molly.

Jeremy shook his head.

"No, I don't think so. You should have seen the way that she looked at them. It was like they were doing something really disgusting."

"Such as?"

"I don't know. Cutting their toenails on the table or something."

They both turned as Carlos came in, his expression interested.

"Who's been cutting their toenails on the table?"

"Nobody," said Jeremy. "I was just using it as an example."

"Well," said Carlos, "when I lived with mum in the Meadows there was this man and he…"

Molly cut across him.

"Not just before dinner, Carlos. Did you get the camp set up all right?"

"Yes, it's great. We found a really good spot. Molly, is it all right if I go back to see them after dinner? Just for an hour or so."

Molly nodded.

"Of course. I expect that you've got a lot to catch up on."

"They were telling me about Sir William. Their dad knows him from some business stuff. Teddy thinks that her dad doesn't really like him."

"Really?" said Jeremy. "Why not?"

"Well, Teddy's mum knows the first Lady Pelham. The one that turned up drunk at that cocktail drinks thing. They met at some charity thing or something. And she said that her mum said that Sir William shouldn't have done it. Left the first Lady Pelham, I mean."

Molly reached past him to take some cutlery out of the drawer.

"Well, sometimes Carlos, marriages do end you know."

"I know but Casper said that this new one is just after Sir William's money. And that he met her in a pub."

Jeremy smiled and took a sip of his wine.

"Don't sound so shocked, Carlos. People have to meet somewhere."

"Yes, but she worked there."

Jeremy suppressed a grin. The young were so judgemental. Bar maids and knights of the realm were not supposed to mix, let alone marry.

"And Teddy's mum said that she was always wearing short skirts and flirting with men," continued Carlos. "She said that she made a bee-line for Sir William." He paused. "What's a bee-line?"

"It's sort of when you go straight for something," said Jeremy.

Carlos nodded. Another new word for his collection. He ought to start writing them down before he forgot them.

"Anyway, he'd been married to the other Lady Pelham for about a hundred years. And when he met this new one, everyone in the village knew about it. Like he didn't even try to hide it or anything. And Sir William's older children hate her."

This last was said with a note of triumph, as though he had proved his point.

Molly laughed.

"Well, it's none of our business. Nobody really knows what goes on in other peoples' families. We shouldn't gossip."

Carlos thought for a moment. She was right. They didn't know what really went on behind closed doors. For instance, he'd never told anybody at school about the time his mother had been ill with flu and hadn't been able to go out and do her cleaning work. For several days he had turned up at school half-starved and been told off for inattention. It was only when the local foodbank put flyers through all the doors on the Meadows that they were able to get a decent meal. Even that had been fraught with worry. As illegal immigrants, they were always flying below the radar. Luckily, on the day that he had presented himself at the door of the foodbank there had been a kindly lady in charge who, recognising real need when she saw it, hadn't asked too many questions. Especially when she'd seen how close to tears he was.

"We're just here to have a nice holiday," continued Molly. "So let's enjoy ourselves." She passed the cutlery to him. "Go and lay the table. I'm sure that we can squeeze another chair out on the balcony."

CHAPTER FIFTEEN

CARLOS WALKED QUIETLY through the grounds, breathing in the night air and looking around him. It was peaceful out here, the only sounds came from the rustle of small animals in the bushes and trees. He paused for a moment and watched as a hedgehog scurried past him. He liked hedgehogs. There was something very purposeful about them. Like, they never looked like they weren't sure where they were going. You wouldn't catch a hedgehog stopping to ask directions. To his left the lights of the hotel glimmered faintly. Behind him crept Aubrey and Vincent, challenging themselves as to who could make the least noise.

He felt his heart warm at the thought of Teddy and Casper staying nearby. Molly and Jeremy had promised Jonathon Beaumont that they would keep an eye on them and in turn he had promised Molly and Jeremy that he would do his best to see that Casper kept out of trouble. The problem was that Casper had a habit of finding trouble before it knew that it was lost, but he'd do his best. He was just glad that they were there at all, given that they very nearly hadn't been. When they were setting up the tents, Teddy had told him that her parents had said at the last minute that she couldn't go after all and she'd had to work really hard to persuade them to change their minds. They definitely wouldn't let her go camping on her own because she was a girl, she said, even though she was seventeen. And they wouldn't let Casper go camping on his own because he couldn't be trusted.

He could see their point about Casper but when he'd asked Teddy why being a girl meant that she couldn't go camping on her own she had said that it was in case she was attacked or something. It had made him think. Like, here he was, walking on his own through the darkness and it had never occurred to him not to. But girls couldn't do that in case a man attacked them. He'd said to Teddy that the chances of anyone being attacked were, like, about a million to one and Teddy had said yes, but what if you were that one? Then she had told him that near where they lived a girl that she was in sixth form with had been attacked in a multi-storey car park. She'd only just passed her driving test which somehow seemed to make it worse. The girl hadn't come back to college and they still hadn't caught the man responsible.

What made a man do something like that, Carlos wondered. Like, did they hate girls or something? But if they hated them, then why didn't they just stay away from them? He blushed suddenly as he remembered some of the crude remarks made about girls by two or three of the boys at college. One thing that one of them had said, he didn't even know what it meant. Only that it sounded revolting. The boy that had said it reminded him of Jed Caparo, the boy who had got him into trouble when he was at school. The boy had the same flinty eyes and sly way of looking around him as Caparo, and the same way of damaging everything he came into contact with. The kind of boy that was best avoided, by girls and boys alike.

Just ahead of him the little copse showed a faint light. Had Casper defied Teddy and lit a fire? He doubted it. Wild and unruly as Casper might be, if Teddy gave an order he generally followed it. She was about the only person that he ever really took any notice of. The light was probably coming from a torch, one of those big camping ones like Jeremy had. He approached the little camp noisily, making loud coughing noises as he walked. He didn't want to frighten them by creeping up on them. As he approached he could see Teddy and Casper sitting on the ground, two big fat candles burning in front of them, eating chocolate. Teddy looked up at him, her small heart-shaped face alight.

"You're here! And you've brought the cats with you! Hello Aubrey."

Carlos looked down on Aubrey and Vincent who had slunk in behind him, and grinned. He hadn't known they were there. Teddy reached over and scooped Aubrey up in her arms. Casper made a lunge for Vincent, who moved swiftly out of the way. He liked Teddy, he had met her before, but he didn't know who this boy was. He'd need to check him out before allowing any contact.

"I thought that you weren't allowed any fires?" said Carlos, remembering his promise to keep Casper out of trouble, and nodding towards the candles.

"It's not a fire," said Casper. "They're candles."

"Anyway," said Teddy. "We've got something to tell you."

Carlos felt his heart sink. Don't say that you're going home already, he thought. You've only just arrived.

"Something that we heard at the hotel," added Casper, holding out a square of chocolate to Vincent who, after inching closer and taking a tentative lick, was discovering that he liked it.

"After you left, we went up to the hotel to wash our faces and clean our teeth." Teddy, Carlos thought, looked particularly pretty in the candlelight. When he had his restaurant he would make sure that every table had candles so that everybody would always look their best. None of this stainless steel and strip lighting industrial look that some chefs went in for. It made everybody look like they'd been worked over in the morgue. His restaurant would have soft lighting and pretty flowers and he would only employ people who smiled... he blinked and brought himself back to the present as Teddy continued. "We promised mum that we would. And the receptionist was really nice and she knew our names and everything. She told us that we could use the bathroom in the Basil suite and gave us the key. They're all named after herbs," she added. "So we went up there and..."

"If I had a hotel I'd name all the rooms after dinosaurs," interrupted Casper. "So there'd be rooms called things like diplodocus or," he thought for a moment. "Maybe after poisoners like Crippen..."

"Shut up, Casp. Anyway, we heard some people talking in the next room," said Teddy. "All the windows were open, and Casper went over and listened. Or, I should say, Casper eavesdropped."

Nothing wrong with that, thought Aubrey, wriggling out of Teddy's arms. How else did anybody find anything out?

"Well, you were just as interested as me," Casper protested.

"Yes, I was," admitted Teddy. "Anyway, the voices were quite low but we could hear what they were saying. And you'll never guess what?"

"No, what?" Carlos dropped down beside her, breathing in the faint perfume from her hair, and accepting the piece of chocolate that she held out to him.

"They were talking about somebody being missing. And," she added breathlessly, "a ransom."

Carlos nodded. He knew what a ransom was. When he had lived in Sao Paulo with his mother there had been a spate of kidnappings, usually the wives or husbands of local politicians who lived in the posh areas. Everybody knew about it but it was rarely reported to the police for fear of harm coming to the victims. Once the money was paid they usually turned up all right. But things like that didn't happen in England, at least, probably only to really important people who were on the television and that, and who, he wondered, was so important at Seton Manor that somebody would pay a ransom for their return? As if reading his thoughts, Teddy continued.

"It's a little boy. Sir William's son. We heard them say his name. Orlando."

"And then," said Casper, "one of them said he'll get the police in and the other one said that he won't."

"What else did they say?"

"That Sir William is going to pay two million pounds to get him back and that they would have to tread carefully."

Carlos looked shocked. He couldn't even imagine how much two million pounds was. And even if he could, why would anybody pay that for Orlando? Surely whoever had taken him was doing everybody a favour. He'd seen Orlando when they had arrived. A sturdy little figure who had stood watching them as they unpacked the car and had then bounced over to them and announced "I am Sir William Pelham's son" before bouncing back off again. Jeremy had merely raised his eyebrows and continued unloading the boot, but Carlos had watched him as he picked up a handful of gravel and took careful aim at a squirrel that was balancing on the branch of a tree.

"Do you know who the people were?" he asked.

Teddy shook her head.

"No, one of them said to keep their voices down and then they closed the window."

"I was going to knock on the door and pretend to be room service," said Casper, his mouth full of chocolate. "But Teddy wouldn't let me."

"Casp," said Teddy, "room service don't turn up in jeans and trainers."

"I was going to say that I was on work experience."

Teddy sighed.

"Well, anyway, we know what room they were in because we looked on the door," she said. "They were in the Parsley suite."

CHAPTER SIXTEEN

CARLOS STIRRED IN his sleep and opened his eyes. A noise from outside had woken him. It sounded like a gun shot. When he had lived in downtown Sao Paulo, the sound of gunshot had been one that was horribly familiar and a signal to all the residents to stay behind closed doors and to keep their mouths shut. There had been several shootings in the Meadows too, usually involving the dealers who had made it one of their home patches. But who would have a gun at Seton Manor? Poachers possibly, if there was anything to poach. Or maybe he was mistaken, maybe it was just a car back-firing.

He wriggled down into the bed and closed his eyes again but it was no good. He was wide awake now. Always a light sleeper since he was a small boy, it took the merest rustle to shake him into wakefulness and once awake he usually stayed awake. When he was in Sao Paulo, to be on high alert had been a necessity. Especially in the place that he had lived with his mother just before they came to England, a block of rundown apartments where locks on rooms were short and violent thieves were rife. But even though the prospect of gangs with knives breaking into his room these days was remote to say the least, the habit of flickering into wakefulness at the slightest disturbance had stayed with him.

Dismissing the noise as unimportant, he settled back against his pillows and let his mind run over the events of yesterday. He'd had a brilliant day and today looked to be even better. He and Teddy and Casper were going to take a picnic down to the village green where a cricket match was due to be played. Molly and Jeremy had said that they might come too. He didn't know anything about cricket other than idle glances when Jeremy was watching it on the television, but it looked quite interesting. Cricket wasn't a game played at Sir Frank Wainwright's. At Sir Frank's the preferred game was rugby, by both boys and girls. Whether or not they played by the rules he had never been quite sure. At Sir Frank's it seemed to involve somebody kicking a ball and then everyone piling in and beating the shit out of each other. Anyway, Teddy seemed to like cricket and that was good enough for him. He had volunteered to make the picnic and had already planned what he was going to put in it. Molly had agreed to run him first thing to the small supermarket in the neighbouring town to get what he needed. He might not know anything about cricket but he knew about food and he was going to make a feast that they would never forget.

He clasped his hands behind his head and thought about his two friends. It was weird what they were saying about that kid Orlando. Who was it, he wondered, that they had overheard talking? If they were the kidnappers they would almost certainly be dangerous. Carlos felt a slight flutter of fear. For all their worldly ways, Teddy and even Casper were innocents. They lived in a world where grown-ups were people to be trusted and the police were always on their side. But somebody who was prepared to take a child, even if that child was the odious Orlando, was a very dangerous person indeed. He would have to warn them to be careful, especially Casper to whom the word caution represented a challenge.

On the other hand, the people that they had overheard talking might not be the actual kidnappers. They might just have heard about it somehow. But it would still be interesting to know who they were. One or both of them must have been staying in the Parsley suite or they wouldn't have had a key to get in there. How, he wondered, could he find out? In the old days, hotel receptionists used to keep a big sort of book on the desk and check people in and out that way, he'd seen it on the old movies that he used to watch on Sunday afternoons with Maria. Nowadays it was all online and even if the receptionist left her post, the computer would almost certainly be password protected. He'd give it some thought. There must be some way to find out.

Feeling a movement by his feet, he sat up straighter and glanced down at the bottom of the bed. Aubrey sat up and looked at him. Carlos smiled and reached down to stroke him.

"Hello Aubrey. I didn't know you were there. Where's Vincent?"

Out, thought Aubrey. Vincent had always been in the habit of taking himself off at odd times and he obviously didn't see any reason to change that now he was on holiday. Aubrey didn't mind. He quite liked being on his own too sometimes and being with Carlos like this, just the two of them, reminded him of the old days when Carlos had first come to live with them.

"I was just thinking," said Carlos, running his hand down Aubrey's back, "about what Teddy and Casper were saying about that Orlando kid and the ransom and everything. I wonder why the police haven't been called?" He thought for a moment. "I expect they're afraid. The kidnapper's probably threatened to kill him or something."

Aubrey padded up the bed and settled his weight on Carlos's chest. Much as he disliked Orlando, he wouldn't actively wish any harm to come to him. He would have a word with Vincent, maybe they should have a scout round. After all, they'd do it if a cat went missing. It was sort of what you had to do, even if it was a cat that you didn't think much of it. Like the time he'd been part of the search party when Pansy went missing. He thought about Pansy for a moment, small and delicate with tiny white tips to her paws, she was a nasty piece of work if ever there was one. She had been forever running to Rupert and Roger, the Siamese who ran the manor, telling tales. Trapped in a neighbour's shed, he had heard a cat crying. He had jumped up and looked in the window and there she was, tucked up in a corner on a pile of old sacking. Part of him, and if he was honest, it was a big part, was tempted to just leave her there and go back and join the others. But he hadn't. He had done the right thing and shown her the way out through the gap in the panel at the back. It was typical of Pansy to go into a strange place without checking the exits first. She had probably fallen asleep and the shed owner had just shut the door as he passed.

Carlos tickled his ears and then wrapped his arms around him and placed him gently to one side.

"I'm thirsty. I'll be back in a minute."

Swinging his legs out of bed Carlos made his way through to the kitchen. The moonlight filtered through the big window, taking off the hard edges and basking everything in a soft glow. Carlos filled a glass with water and wandered back through to the sitting room. The balcony door stood slightly ajar for the cats to come in and out, and he could feel the cool of the dawn drifting in. It was a welcome relief after the heat of the night. Sipping at his water, he stepped outside, feeling the delicious coolness of the tiles against his bare feet. He looked around him at the trees and shrubs and the long green lawns. It was beautiful here. His mother would have loved it. It looked like the pictures in the English magazines that her employers gave her when they'd finished reading them. It was the kind of place that he would have taken her for a holiday when he got rich. Or, if he got rich enough, maybe even bought for her.

He glanced down at the swimming pool. There, in the centre, was a large star-shaped thing. He leaned over the balcony rail and looked more closely. The thing was a body, arms and legs out, head down, floating in the water.

CHAPTER SEVENTEEN

CARLOS SAT ON the sofa, a cat tucked in on either side of him. The early morning sun was just rising and it looked like it was going to be another hot day. His earlier happy mood had completely evaporated and now he felt like he had that time he caught flu. Sort of cold and shaky and like he might start crying or something. Every time he stood up, his legs felt like cotton wool and he had to sit down again. From outside he could hear the sound of police talking into radios and the thrum of engines as vehicles came and went. He clutched Aubrey to him and buried his face in his fur. Teddy had already messaged him to say that their father had heard the news on the local radio while he was getting ready for work and would be picking them up shortly. He looked up as Jeremy came in.

"Are you all right, Carlos?"

No, he wasn't all right, thought Aubrey. None of them were. A man had been found dead in the hotel swimming pool and a not very jolly holiday this was turning out to be. He sighed and tucked his head under his paw. Yesterday had been a great day. Before spending time with Teddy and Casper down in the copse he and Vincent had enjoyed a fine old time exploring the grounds. They had even found an old tumbled down building, a sort of brick thing covered in ivy. Vincent said that he thought it might have been a pig stye although how he knew these things Aubrey had no idea. There were no pigs in it now, though he wouldn't have minded if there had been. Vincent had said that pigs were good fun, as long as you didn't annoy them. Although, thought Aubrey, you could say that about anybody. Even Jeremy had been known to get cross occasionally, usually when he realised that he'd forgotten to fill the car with petrol and was running late for a meeting he had to get to.

He glanced across at Vincent. He had been particularly quiet since he had come in this morning. Almost as though he was worried about something. In fact he had hardly spoken a word.

"All right, Vin?"

Vincent nodded, his expression inscrutable. Aubrey regarded him for a moment and then closed his eyes. Whatever it was, Vincent would tell him when he felt like it. And with all this palaver going on he felt quite worn out. Time for a little nap.

Jeremy crossed the room and sat down next to them. For a moment they all sat in silence.

"What did the police say?" asked Carlos at last.

"Not very much," admitted Jeremy. "I guess everybody will have to be interviewed."

Carlos suddenly felt brighter. If everybody had to be interviewed then that meant that Teddy and Casper couldn't go home, at least not just yet. Please, he prayed silently, let them be interviewed last.

"Anything else?" he asked.

Jeremy shrugged.

"Not really."

He thought for a moment about the surly police officer who looked as if he had taken it as a personal affront that he had been dragged out to investigate the sudden appearance of a dead body. Perhaps, he thought, in a sudden effort to be fair, he had just been about to go off duty and had been looking forward to going home and putting his feet up. But be that as it may, his responses had been practically monosyllabic to say the least.

Apart from telling Jeremy to go back inside, he had said almost nothing. He turned his head as Molly came through from the bathroom.

"I wonder if anybody has broken the news to Sir William yet?" She sat down opposite Jeremy and Carlos and glanced out of the window where scene of crime officers were busy going about their business, their protective clothing adding a ghastly sci-fi effect to the scene. "It's so dreadful. I wonder how it happened? I mean, do you think it was an accident? That he had been drinking and fell in or something?" She paused. "Supposing that it is a he, that is."

Jeremy reached across Carlos and stroked Aubrey.

"I think it was a man but you're right, it could be a woman. As for it being an accident, who knows? There was definitely what looked like blood in the water."

He yawned, feeling suddenly not so much tired as totally exhausted, which was hardly surprising given the events of the last hour or so. When Carlos had shaken him awake to tell him that he thought there was a dead body floating in the swimming pool, he had thought that Carlos was dreaming. When he had first come to them after his mother had been killed he had suffered terrible nightmares, often waking everybody by shouting and calling out. In those early days Jeremy had frequently found himself sitting by Carlos's bed and talking quietly to him until he had calmed down and gone back to sleep. But it had been a long time since there had been any recurrence and this happening tonight had come as a bit of a surprise.

He had felt the light touch on his shoulder and had woken from sleep, rubbing his eyes, to see Carlos standing over him, his dark eyes huge in his pale face. The little digital clock read five thirty. Molly was still asleep and he had tried to focus as Carlos told him in a heavy whisper about what he thought he had seen in the swimming pool. He had got reluctantly out of bed, careful not to wake Molly, and beckoned Carlos to follow him. He would have to go and look to reassure him and then they could all go back to sleep. He had padded sleepily through the sitting room and out on to the balcony, joined by Aubrey and Vincent who had now turned up again, and then stared in disbelief at the scene in front of him. At first he'd thought that it must be some sort of prank, that it was somebody's idea of a joke to put a tailor's dummy in the water. But he could see, even from the balcony that those hands, that head, belonged to a person.

When he had telephoned the police, they had also been inclined to think it was some sort of practical joke but had wearily assured him that they would take a ride out just to double-check. On arrival they had moved from amused tolerance of a confused tourist who had possibly had one too many, to cranking up the whole sudden death machine within seconds.

"I wonder who it is?" asked Molly. "A guest at the hotel, do you think?"

"Maybe," Jeremy agreed. "Or it might just be a trespasser. Somebody who wandered into the grounds. What is it, Carlos?" He glanced sharply across at him. Years of teaching had developed in him a radar which beamed in when a teenager was holding something back. It was something to do with the slight shift in expression, a tenseness in the body and the inability to look anybody in the eye. "What are you worried about?"

Carlos hesitated and looked across at Molly. She smiled at him.

"What's the matter Carlos? You can tell us, whatever it is."

"It's that kid. Orlando. Sir William's little boy."

"What about him?" asked Molly. "Has he been annoying you?"

She wouldn't be surprised if he had. The boy had an irritating habit of hanging around the guests and staring at them, usually while stuffing his face with sweets.

"He's been kidnapped." Carlos spoke quickly and quietly and then held his breath, as if afraid that somebody else had heard.

"He's been what?" Jeremy stared at him.

"Kidnapped," repeated Carlos. "By a kidnapper."

"How do you know?" asked Molly.

Carlos hesitated and chewed at the side of his mouth. But Teddy and Casper hadn't done anything wrong. They just happened to hear some people talking. He wasn't dropping them in it by telling Molly and Jeremy. Dropping people in it was about the worst teenage offence you could commit. He hadn't even dropped Marcus Worth in it when some dinner money had been taken from a blazer pocket. Initially all eyes had turned on him as the newest kid to the school, but he had actually seen Marcus dipping his slimy little hand into a blazer hanging on the back of a chair. While denying that he had committed the crime he had kept his mouth shut about Marcus and waited with an increasing sense of dread for the inevitable retribution to fall on him.

Fortunately for him, Marcus, being the greedy little sod that he was, did it again and this time not only was he seen by the victim but had the misfortune to pick the blazer owned by Kermit, the biggest boy in the school who habitually dyed his hair green. On the basis of the school's code of honour, namely, never nick from your own, Marcus had received due punishment by way of a good kicking from Kermit and another boy. Justice was rough at Sir Frank Wainwrights, but it was swift. Carlos had received his reward for not grassing by suddenly finding himself accepted. One boy had even offered him the use of his felt tip pens in geography, which he had stolen from a shop on the high street, and offered to steal a similar set for Carlos. He'd refused on the basis that Molly or Jeremy might ask him where he'd got them from, but he had appreciated the offer.

He took a deep breath.

"Teddy and Casper heard some people talking about it at the hotel. They were in the room next door using the bathroom and they heard them talking. In the Parsley suite," he added.

"They probably misunderstood," said Jeremy. "The people were probably talking about a television programme or something. If a kidnapping had really happened then surely everybody would know about it."

Carlos shook his head. There were some things that he was more knowledgeable about than Molly and Jeremy, and this was one of them.

"No. If somebody gets kidnapped you have to keep it quiet, otherwise the person who's been kidnapped might get hurt."

Jeremy looked at him. Carlos was possibly right, and it would explain the tense atmosphere up at the hotel yesterday.

"What else did Teddy and Casper hear?"

"The kidnappers are asking for two million pounds."

CHAPTER EIGHTEEN

THERE WAS A moment's silence while Molly and Jeremy thought about the enormity of the sum of money being asked.

"I suppose," said Jeremy eventually, "if you're going to do something like that, you might as well make it worth your while. I mean, it's not worth going to prison for the sake of a few thousand quid. But two million... well, whoever it is, they're not mucking about, that's for sure."

"Do you think that Sir William has got that kind of money?" asked Molly.

"I should think so. I mean, you've only got to look at this place," said Jeremy, waving his hand around. "Talk about no expense spared."

They jumped at a sudden loud rapping on the apartment door.

"I'll get it," said Molly. She opened the apartment door and the burly policeman that Jeremy had spoken to earlier walked in. He looked round at them, a faint expression of suspicion on his face.

"Which one of you found the body?"

Nil points for sensitivity, thought Jeremy.

"I did," said Carlos. "Well, I didn't exactly find it..."

The police officer gave him a sour look.

"Well you either found it or you didn't. Which is it?"

Molly moved across to Carlos and put a hand on his shoulder. She gave a gentle squeeze.

"We've all had a bit of a shock," she said. "Why don't I fetch us all some coffee and biscuits?"

The police officer wiped a hand over his eyes and nodded.

"That would be very welcome. Do you mind if I sit down?"

Jeremy nodded and watched as the man sank on to a small easy chair which gave a tiny creak of protest as he lowered his bulk on to the seat.

"It's been a rough night," the police officer said. "A hit and run, a break-in at the local pub and a fight down on the village green. And now this. Round these parts we can go for months with nothing more exciting happening than a bit of vandalism to the bus shelter. We've already had to call in extra officers and it's not even mid-morning yet."

"Has anybody told Sir William what's happened?" asked Molly, calling through from the kitchen.

"Officers are up at the Manor now. I don't envy them. I wouldn't fancy breaking it to him."

"Do you know who the person is?" asked Jeremy.

The police officer shook his head.

"Not at present. I've phoned in but nobody has reported any missing person. He looks to be fully clothed so there might be something to identify him there."

"Was it an accident?"

"Difficult to tell at this stage." The officer thought for a moment. "There's blood in the water but we'll have more info later, when the doc's finished his examination." He paused. "There was a big twenty-first birthday party in the village hall last night. From all accounts they were still going hard at it in the early hours. My guess is that it's a local who had a bit too much to drink and fancied an early swim. There was quite a spate of it at one time, when the pool was first constructed. But whoever it is, Sir William won't be best pleased."

"I should think not," said Jeremy. "It's not exactly got the hallmarks of a good publicity stunt. Who wants to go to a hotel where a body's been found in the pool?"

The policeman smiled suddenly.

"You're not wrong there, sir. Of course, Sir William has had a fair share of trouble with locals in the past over various things." He took the mug of steaming coffee from Molly and wrapped his large hands around it. "Sir William is not exactly what you'd call popular in these parts."

"Why is that?" asked Molly, sitting down on the sofa. "I thought that he was rather charming."

The police officer considered for a moment and let his face relax. It made him look, thought Jeremy, much more human. Less the granite faced plod of popular imagination and more like a man who just wants to finish his shift and go home.

"Well, he can be when it suits him," he conceded. He took a large gulp of coffee which seemed to revive him and he momentarily closed his eyes in appreciation. "But when it doesn't... well, he's not a man that you'd want to cross."

Jeremy thought about it for a moment. He wasn't surprised. You didn't get to be as rich and successful as Sir William by being soft.

"What about Seton Manor?" asked Jeremy. "Did the locals mind it being turned into a hotel?"

The police officer nodded.

"There was a lot of opposition at the time. Meetings in the village hall and so on. Matters got very heated at one point and there was a lot of name-calling. On both sides. And his separating from the first Lady Pelham didn't go down at all well either. She did a lot for charity and so on. Ah, well." He drained his coffee and fished in his pocket for his notebook. He turned to Carlos.

"Now then young man. Suppose you tell me exactly what happened."

CHAPTER NINETEEN

JEREMY LEANED BACK and took a sip of his coffee. He grimaced and put it back down on the table. It had gone cold by now and, anyway, he didn't really feel like drinking coffee this morning. If it wasn't so early, he'd have a stiff whisky instead. Carlos looked across at him.

"Do you think that I should have told him?"

For a moment Jeremy didn't answer. He knew what Carlos was talking about, and so did Molly. He glanced at her before speaking.

"I don't know, Carlos." He spoke slowly, measuring his words. "But all three of us know about it, not just you, and none of us said anything."

"The thing is," said Molly, "if we told the police and then some harm came to the boy, how would we feel then? I think that it's up to Sir William and Lady Pelham to do what they think is for the best."

Jeremy nodded.

"I agree to some extent, Moll. But harm might come to him anyway and how would that make us feel? I mean, as kids go, he's not exactly an attractive prospect but that's probably his parents fault. None of us would actually wish him any harm." He paused and thought for a moment. "And for all we know, things might be connected. I mean, it's more than a bit odd. A boy gets kidnapped and then a body turns up in the swimming pool."

Carlos looked from one to the other.

"Why don't we tell Sir William that we know and see what happens?"

Jeremy looked at Carlos and nodded.

"That's not a bad idea at all, Carlos. Perhaps we could persuade him to tell the police. I mean, I don't suppose that this sort of thing happens every day but they must have some procedures or done training or something for this type of situation. But I don't think that we can just do nothing, not now this," he gestured towards the open balcony door, "has happened."

Carlos reached into his pocket as his phone began to vibrate and glanced down. His face brightened.

"It's from Teddy. She said can they come and wait for their father here?"

"Yes, of course," said Molly. "Tell them to come straight over."

Carlos jumped up.

"I'll go and meet them. Help them carry their stuff."

Molly and Jeremy watched as he bounded out of the room. Molly turned to Jeremy.

"I know that Carlos wouldn't agree, but I can't help feeling glad that Teddy and Casper are going home. And," she added reluctantly, "I think that we should go home too, as soon as the police allow people to leave."

Jeremy nodded.

"I guess so. Finding a dead body in the hotel swimming pool has rather taken the shine off things. I don't think I'd fancy a swim in there again in a hurry. In fact the very thought of it makes me feel slightly sick. God, this was supposed to be a relaxing holiday and now it's all gone a bit Agatha Christie."

Molly smiled. Reading and re-reading Agatha Christie had long been a habit of Jeremy's, ever since he was thirteen and had first discovered her books. His mother had given him a copy of The Murder Of Roger Ackroyd when he was off school with a throat infection and he had been hooked ever since. He read other crime writers and enjoyed them but he always returned to Agatha, particularly in times of stress. In recent years he had even taken to collecting early editions which were still available at car boot sales and village fairs, and which he displayed on a shelf in his study.

"Did she ever have a kidnapping in one of her plots?" Molly asked.

Jeremy thought for a moment. He couldn't recall offhand, but there had definitely been an unidentified dead body turning up in one book, although that had been in a library. In fact now he thought about it, the book was called The Body In The Library. Like lots of her titles, it told you exactly what you were in for. And all the better for it, in his opinion. He let his mind wander over the range of her plots and characters. Had there ever been a murder method that she hadn't used? She'd definitely had strangling, poisoning and shooting. What else was there? He could always Google it…

"Jeremy, are you listening to me?" asked Molly.

"Yes, sorry Moll. I was just thinking about Agatha's plots. But, tempting though it is to think that the body in the pool is part of some sort of complicated drama in which Hercule Poirot will turn up and denounce the villain, I suspect that it's much more mundane than that. The police officer is probably right, it's probably a local who had too much to drink and hit his head when he dived in. When I was a lad, we often used to go swimming in the local river. Usually after we'd drunk some strong lager on the bank. It was a wonder really that no harm ever came to us. Unlike this poor soul," he added.

"What about the kidnap?"

"I don't know. A strong part of me thinks that we really should tell the police what we know. Or what we think we know. Remember, this is only what Teddy and Casper think that they overheard. They might have got it totally wrong."

"What about Carlos's idea of talking to Sir William first?"

Jeremy nodded.

"That's probably the best plan."

He turned as Carlos, Teddy and Casper burst into the apartment, dragging their tents and rucksacks behind them. He was struck suddenly by how young they all were. They radiated that high octane energy that is impossible to recapture later in life. Not that he'd ever tried very hard, he had to admit. Apart from the annual ritual of joining a gym and then not going after the first month, a round of golf was generally the most he undertook by way of exercise.

"Casper heard Sir William talking to the police," said Carlos, slightly breathless as the three of them tumbled onto the sofa. They had, thought Jeremy, run all the way from the copse. They must have to get here this quickly. He turned to Casper who had jumped up from the sofa and taken up position in front of the balcony, feet apart, head held high and his hands clasped behind his back.

"Stop showing off, Casp," said Teddy. She turned to Jeremy and Molly. "He was eavesdropping. Again."

"I heard them," Casper rushed in, anxious that Teddy was about to steal his thunder. "They said that Sir William had to check to see if any guests were missing and he had to come out here and identify the body."

"Only if he knows who it is," said Molly. "Anyway, what were you doing up at the hotel?"

"When dad rang and said that he was coming to collect us, I legged it over there to find out what had happened. They were talking by the window." He turned suddenly and looked out across the balcony as the unmistakeable sound of Sir William's voice floated upwards. "They're here now."

CHAPTER TWENTY

ALMOST UNCONSCIOUSLY THE little group made a collective movement towards the French window, keeping themselves out of view from the scene below. They could hear the voices of Sir William and several police officers, Sir William's rich and confident, the officers more muted. Dropping on to his stomach, Casper crawled commando style on to the balcony and peered over. He twisted his head back towards them, his face red with excitement.

"He's leaning over and looking at the body. It's covered in some plastic sheet thing and they're pulling it back." He paused and crept a little closer to the edge.

"Casper," Jeremy began. "I don't really think…"

Casper suddenly wriggled backwards and sat up. He stared at Jeremy, his eyes wide.

"I know who it is. I saw his face."

There was a moment's silence.

"Who?" said Molly, her voice barely more than a whisper.

"That handy bloke from the hotel. The one who does the driving and gardening and stuff. He came to look at our camp to make sure that we weren't making a mess. Which we weren't," he added virtuously.

"You mean Guido," said Jeremy slowly. "Remember Moll, he was the one who took the first Lady Pelham home that night."

Molly nodded.

"Yes. I could hardly forget."

Casper crawled out to the balcony again and peered over. Almost immediately he reversed back and jumped to his feet.

"Quick, get back. He's coming up here. Sir William is coming up here."

The five of them rushed to take up position, each assuming an air of innocent unconcern. Falling in with the mood, Aubrey and Vincent flopped down on the rug and pretended to be asleep. Taking her time, Molly got up and answered the door to Sir William's knock.

"I'm so sorry to disturb you."

Sir William walked in and looked around at each of them in turn. He didn't, thought Jeremy, look very sorry. They might be paying for the privilege of staying in one of the apartments but Sir William was still the lord of the manor and as such entitled to go where he pleased, when he pleased. He was, Jeremy noticed, dressed elegantly as always. This time in smart chinos and a crisply ironed pale blue shirt, with the cuffs turned up just above the wrist to reveal a heavy gold watch. On his feet he wore brown loafers of rich leather with no socks. A faint scent of expensive cologne wafted towards them. God, did nothing ever ruffle the man? He'd just been informed that a dead body had turned up in his pool and he still looked like an advertisement for a cruise holiday. The kind of cruise holiday that required a second mortgage. Jeremy looked down ruefully at his own tatty jeans and baggy T shirt which he'd pulled on in a hurry while waiting for the police. Ah well, you'd either got it or you hadn't. And he hadn't. But he did have Molly, Carlos, Aubrey and Vincent which, really, was about as much as he wanted so that was all right.

"I gather," Sir William continued, "that one of you discovered the body. Please accept my heartfelt apology. It has hardly been a propitious beginning to your holiday."

Casper nudged Carlos in the ribs. Carlos jumped and cleared his throat.

"Sir William, it was me. I saw it first and told Jeremy. And then Jeremy reported it to the police."

Jeremy stood up. Sitting down while Sir William was standing had felt strangely uncomfortable, as if he was at some kind of disadvantage.

"That's right," he said. Avoiding the eye of any of the other listeners, he continued. "Do you know who it is yet?"

Sir William nodded.

"It is Guido. My general factotum."

Carlos felt his mouth drop open slightly. His general what?

"We're very sorry, it must have been a terrible shock for you," said Molly. "Did he have any family do you know?"

Sir William shook his head.

"None that I'm aware of. He answered an advertisement two years ago and has been here ever since. Before that I understand that he was something to do with the military. He was very good," he added. "Could turn his hand to all sorts of things. All sorts."

"Were the police able to tell you what happened?" asked Jeremy. "Oh," he gestured towards a chair. "Please do sit down."

Sir William sank down in the chair that the police officer had occupied earlier and stretched his long legs in front of him.

"They appear to be unsure at present as to whether or not he was dead before he hit the water. There will, of course, be a full post-mortem."

Jeremy, who had remained standing, nodded. He exchanged glances with Molly.

"You three," said Molly, looking at the three teenagers on the sofa. "Why don't you go outside and amuse yourselves? I'm sure that the police won't mind you doing that. But don't go too far."

Teddy opened her mouth to protest and then shut it again as Carlos gave her hand a quick squeeze. Molly, Jeremy and Sir William watched as the three of them stood up and left the room, Casper glancing behind him as he went.

"Sir William," began Jeremy, and then faltered. He'd never been called on to find the words to tell somebody that he knew their son had been kidnapped, and he wasn't sure where to start.

Molly, sensing his hesitation, interrupted.

"Sir William, we may well be wrong about this but rumour has it that your youngest son, Orlando, has, well, disappeared."

Sir William stared at her, his eyes narrowed.

"And what makes you say that?"

"The children seem to think that they overheard something," said Jeremy. He felt suddenly flustered. He wasn't sure why he'd called them children. It was some sort of protective instinct. "Of course, they've probably got it wrong."

Sir William pressed his lips tightly together and breathed in through his nostrils.

"No, they haven't got it wrong," he said at last. "We have been instructed not to inform the police. We are waiting for further information as to where to deposit the money."

"But Sir William, surely…," began Molly.

He turned to her, his expression fierce, and raised a hand, palm outward.

"I know what you're going to say, Mrs Goodman. But you don't understand." He paused and swallowed hard. "I love my son very much. I could not bear any harm to come to him. He and Bridie are all I live for. The ransom requested is a very large amount, but I have the money."

For a moment there was silence and then Sir William continued.

"Where did the children hear this?"

"At the hotel," said Jeremy. "Apparently it was some people talking in the Parsley suite."

Sir William stared at him.

"The Parsley suite? But that is where my eldest son Jacob is staying."

CHAPTER TWENTY-ONE

AUBREY AND VINCENT watched from the balcony as Sir William strode away, his head down and his hands pushed into his pockets, clearly deep in thought. Without speaking they took a graceful leap and landed four square on the lawn by the swimming pool. The body had been removed and the police officers were packing away now, although the area had been cordoned off with blue and white tape. Vincent turned to Aubrey, his gold neck tag glittering in the sun, rich against his dark fur. It had been put there by his previous owners and he never seemed to mind it, unlike Aubrey who steadfastly refused to wear anything round his neck, and chewed off any collars as soon as he was out of view. Molly and Jeremy had long since given up buying them, especially since he'd been micro-chipped.

"Where do you fancy today, Aubsie?"

Aubrey thought for a moment. They had covered most of the grounds already. There was only the other side of the copse where Teddy and Casper had set up camp that they hadn't really explored. He turned his head in that direction. He felt the heat of the sun on his fur and lifted his face to the sky. It was obvious that they would be going home again soon so they might as well make the most of the time that they had left here.

"Over to the copse?" he suggested.

Vincent nodded and together they set off, keeping to the cover of the trees, as much out of habit as anything else. It was unlikely these days that they would be attacked by anything, especially when they were together, but you could never tell. As Aubrey took care to remind himself from time to time, a careless cat is a vulnerable cat.

Emerging from the other side of the copse was a narrow lane at the end of which stood a small red-brick cottage, the downstairs windows flung open. Creeping slowly forward, they neared the building, each of them making as little noise as possible. While curiosity often got the better of them, they had no intention of letting it be the cause of their early demise. Jumping on to the windowsill they peered in. The room was small but nicely furnished, with the kind of large squishy, slightly shabby, chairs that both of them could envisage making themselves comfortable on. The fireplace, carved oak with a small mirror inset, was brightly polished and on the mantelpiece a jug of wild flowers gave off the scent of summer. In one corner of the room a woman stood looking at some sort of book which she had pulled off the bookshelf, her grey hair ineffectively pinned up so that strands straggled on to her shoulders and neck. As they watched she reached up and pushed some of it back into the clips that held it in place.

Crossing the room Elizabeth Pelham sat down and spread the book open on her lap. Reaching down, she picked up a glass that had been standing in the grate and swirled the ice around before taking a big gulp. Aubrey craned his neck slightly. He could see that the book she was holding was one of those books with pictures in it. Molly and Jeremy had some that were quite old, as was this one by the look of it. Molly and Jeremy's books had been given to them by their parents and occasionally, usually on a winter night over a bottle of wine, they sat and looked at them. Sometimes he sat on one of their laps and looked with them. He always enjoyed it, even though he had no idea who the people in the pictures were. Suddenly Elizabeth glanced up and saw them.

"Hello cats." She spoke in a calm tone, as though the arrival of two unknown cats on her windowsill looking in at her was an everyday occurrence. "Are you real?"

She leaned forward slightly and peered at them.

Sometimes," she continued, sitting back and sipping at her drink as she talked, "I have animals come to visit me and sometimes people. I had a horse once, although he didn't come in through the window. Of course, I know that they're imaginary. But better imaginary friends than none at all."

Aubrey and Vincent looked at each other. Clearly she wasn't hostile. Possibly bonkers, but not hostile. Moving carefully they jumped down on to the cottage floor and walked towards her. Breathing great gusts of gin over them she brought the book down so that they could see it. She pointed with a thin finger to a picture of a group of figures standing in front of what looked like Seton Manor. A woman stood with a child on either side of her while she held a baby in her arms. Behind them, tall and smiling, stood a man, his eyes bright and his hair just silvering at the edges.

"That was taken not long after Emily was born." She tightened her grip on her glass as if for security. "Happier times."

She flipped the page over and peered down at the next image which showed people with drinks in their hands and several tables laden with food.

"That one was taken at a birthday party we held for my mother-in-law. Well, I say we, but of course I was the one that did all the work. There were no staff at Seton Manor in those days, although we did have a cleaner that came in two mornings a week." She sighed. "Eileen. She was a dear woman, I liked her a lot. She always stood by me. She's gone to live with her daughter in Australia now." She sighed and looked thoughtful. "She was the first one to tell me about Bridie. Poor thing. She was so upset but she said that it was the talk of the village and it was better that I heard it from her. Apparently a number of people had witnessed William visiting Bridie and naturally lost no time in drawing their own conclusions. Visiting being a euphemism, of course."

Aubrey moved closer and jumped up on to the arm of her chair. He had no idea what a euphemism was but she looked like she needed a bit of comfort. Reaching out, she began to stroke him.

"That night, the birthday party night," she continued, "William just turned up when all the preparation was done and then stood around chatting. I didn't mind really, his mother wasn't bad, as mothers-in-law go. And she was very good with the children when they were little, always willing to lend a hand. Father-in-law was a different kettle of fish altogether." She paused and took another sip of her drink. "I wonder why we say kettle of fish?"

Aubrey thought about it. He'd never heard of a kettle of fish before but it sounded good. Elizabeth sniffed and jabbed a finger at a man in the picture who stood next to his wife, his belligerent chin jutting out and his mouth open as he addressed the small group in front of him.

"That's him. He was horrible. Always had to be right. Always knew best. What do they call it these days? Mansplaining or something. That was him. Always mansplaining. And he was a bully." She paused. "I will say for William, philanderer that he might have been, he was never really a bully. I suppose," she added sadly, "he didn't need to be. He always got what he wanted anyway. And in the beginning, at the start of our marriage, I gave way to him because I wanted to. I wanted to make him happy. Later, it was just easier."

She drained her glass and flipped the book to the last page.

"And that," she said sourly, "is the tart. William doesn't know that I have this picture. I found it in his car while we were still married. It must have dropped from a pocket. He was such a fool. I always knew of course when he was having his little dalliances. He used to start going to the gym and wearing fancy drawers. He never wore them for me. Apparently it didn't matter if I saw his baggy old Y-fronts. But at least he never paraded his squalid little affairs in front of me, he gave me that dignity. Until the tart came along. Even before Eileen told me about her, I knew that something was up of course. All the usual signs were there but Bridie was different. I could just sense it. Right from the beginning he didn't seem to care what I thought or who knew about it." She sighed. "I don't know what she promised him that the others didn't, but whatever it was it worked. And after that, everything changed."

She smiled down at Vincent who had settled himself comfortably on the rug in front of her.

"Now you might not know this, but once a woman is divorced everything changes. It's almost as though she becomes invisible. Suddenly she's left off guest lists, friends stop dropping round, people start avoiding her. Especially the married ones. It's as if," she thought for a moment. "As though a divorced woman is some kind of threat, something to avoid. Not divorced men though, I've noticed. Divorced men always seem to have their friends wives clucking around them, trying to pair them up with somebody. I've done it myself. But a divorced woman is a danger. She might try to steal their husbands away, you see." She laughed suddenly. "As if. Apart from my age, frankly most of my so-called friends husbands are rather past their best. And that's putting it kindly. Anyway, I'm done with men."

CHAPTER TWENTY-TWO

ELIZABETH STRUGGLED TO her feet and dropped the album on her chair. Crossing the room, she poured more gin from the bottle that stood on the little coffee table. Picking up the empty tonic can she shook it and shrugged. She turned and stared out through the open window, her hands resting on the window sill and her sad eyes taking in the beautiful summer day outside. Spotting her from the branch of a tree, a blackbird began his alarm call. When she spoke, her voice was soft and low.

"The funny thing is that I minded the boy being born more than I minded William getting married again. In a strange way, that hardly impacted on me. I knew that I'd lost him by then, you see. The irony is that he divorced me, not the other way round. He wanted it done quickly, and I just agreed. Unreasonable behaviour, I think it was. I didn't bother to read any of the documents, I just signed what I was told to sign and that was that. My life, the way I lived, it was all gone anyway. What was the point of arguing? He promised to provide me with somewhere to live and an income if I didn't make a fuss so I went along with it. In some ways it seemed like a sort of dream. As though I'd fallen through a crack in reality." She paused and her mouth tightened. "But the child, I did mind. The fact that the child of the tart is a half-brother to my own children, that he shares their blood and DNA, fills me with fury. Apart from anything else, he is such an odious little bastard."

Well, she wasn't wrong there thought Aubrey. That reminded him, odious little bastard that Orlando might be, he was still missing. He must talk to Vincent about it, especially if they were going home soon. Elizabeth turned back to face them.

"Now, I know that you two might think it odd that I have placed the tart's image in my book of memories." She fell silent for a moment and then continued. "But there is a reason. When I am gone, my children will have these albums. I want to remind them, to leave them in no doubt, as to who it was that broke up our home. While William and I might not have had the most passionate of marriages in recent years, one has to ask who does when they get to our sort of ages? But we got on well enough. We'd had our children, we had a nice home, enough money. More than enough money. A decent social life. I was prepared to turn a blind eye to whatever he got up to behind my back. And then the tart turned up. Just look at her."

She picked up the album from where she'd dropped it on the chair and leaned over to show them. Obligingly, Aubrey and Vincent looked. The picture before them showed a young woman leaning over a bar, smiling straight into the camera. The neck of her frilled blouse showed just a trace of cleavage and her hair was piled up artistically on the top of her head, several loose strands trailing winningly around her face and neck. The same hairstyle as the former Lady Pelham but worlds apart in effect. Elizabeth slammed the album shut and clasped it to her chest. Sinking down into the chair again she leaned back and closed her eyes. The album slipped from her grasp and slid down her lap. Aubrey nudged Vincent.

"Might as well check the place out while we're here."

Vincent nodded and followed him through the kitchen door which stood ajar. A large crate filled with empty green glass bottles stood in one corner and a line of smeared glasses were ranged along the draining board. A cupboard door hung open revealing two tins of baked beans and a carton of vegetable soup. The whole room had an empty, stale feeling as though nobody lingered long in there. Not like their kitchen at home, thought Aubrey. Their kitchen at home always had somebody in and out of it and the kitchen table was generally the place where the important decisions were made.

"Upstairs?" he said.

"Might as well while we're here,"

Together they slipped back through the kitchen door and made for the stairs. Reaching the small landing they stopped and turned as the rattle of a key sounded at the front door. Creeping slowly back down, Aubrey and Vincent watched through the bannisters as a tall man strode through the narrow hall and into the sitting room. Leaning over, Sir William shook Elizabeth by the shoulder. She opened her eyes and glared at him.

"Wake up, Elizabeth. I want to talk to you."

Elizabeth struggled upright and pushed him away.

"What are you doing here? I don't recall inviting you."

Sir William stood back and raised his eyebrows slightly.

"I don't need an invitation. I own this place. In case you've forgotten, I am your landlord."

Elizabeth narrowed her eyes.

"I'm hardly likely to forget. Anyway, what do you want."

Sir William sat down in the chair opposite her and tipped his head to one side as he regarded her, his expression grave.

"Why do you do this, Elizabeth? Why do you get yourself in this state?"

Elizabeth sat up straighter and pushed a strand of hair away from her eyes.

"What do you care? Anyway, I thought it would suit you. The sooner I die the sooner you can sell this place."

Sir William smiled, a thin stretching of the lips that held no humour.

"I don't need to wait for you to die. I can sell this place whenever I choose."

For a moment they sat in angry silence then Sir William leaned forward, his hands clasped between his knees, and attempted a conciliatory smile.

"I came to tell you that there has been a death at Seton Manor. Guido has drowned in the swimming pool."

"Oh dear."

Elizabeth's face remained impassive. Sir William frowned and continued.

"That is not all."

Elizabeth remained silent.

"Orlando has... gone missing."

"Really?" she said at last. "I wouldn't have thought that he'd be difficult to find. He's hardly inconspicuous."

Sir William drew a deep breath and pressed his hands more closely together.

"I find this very difficult to say, Elizabeth. Very difficult indeed. You were my wife for many years and you are the mother of three of my children." He paused. "Is it possible that you have any idea where Orlando might be?"

Elizabeth raised her eyebrows and lifted her chin, a delicate arching that gave a sudden glimpse of the undoubted beauty that she had once been. Before the gin and sorrow had taken its toll.

"What on earth makes you think that I know anything about it?"

"Then you won't mind if I search the cottage, will you?"

"Actually William, I would mind. I would mind very much. The fact that you own this cottage does not give you the right to unlimited access and I would thank you not to just let yourself in whenever it pleases."

Sir William stood up and looked down at her, his expression one of contempt mixed with pity.

"Be that as it may, I intend to search this place from top to bottom."

Without waiting for a response he strode from the room. Silently Aubrey and Vincent slipped past him as he began to climb the stairs. Conscious that something had just brushed his legs he turned but there was nothing there.

In the kitchen, Elizabeth pulled open the fridge door and removed a large packet of sweets. Smiling, she dipped her hand in the bag.

CHAPTER TWENTY-THREE

AUBREY AND VINCENT padded quickly back through the copse and towards the hotel. They had no fears about gaining access. There was always a way in if you were a cat. In any event, it was high summer, doors and windows would be open all over the place. Aubrey glanced at his friend as they ran. He was such a good mate. He had agreed immediately to look for Orlando and had suggested that they start with the hotel and work outwards.

Ahead of them they could see three police cars parked at the front. Aubrey turned to Vincent. They both knew from experience that where there were police cars, there was also chaos. And where there was chaos there were often opportunities.

"Still up for it?"

"Course."

Together they sidled up to the front door which stood propped open, and slipped round it. In the reception area the receptionist sat red-eyed behind her desk while a large plain clothed police officer stood taking notes.

"No, honestly. I really don't know anything about him. He just kept himself to himself. He didn't mix with the rest of the staff. I mean, we'd say good morning and so on but that was about it. I used to see him about the place but he never stopped for a chat." The receptionist fumbled in her pocket for a tissue and wiped her nose. "I'm sorry. This has all been such a shock. Lady Pelham is beside herself."

The police officer flipped his notebook shut.

"All right, I shan't trouble you anymore. If you think of anything, please get in touch." He fished in his pocket and took out a card. "Keep it somewhere safe."

He turned as another police officer came through a side door and walked towards him.

"All right, mate? How's it going?"

The first officer glanced down at the receptionist who was now fishing about in her desk drawer for a new pack of tissues.

"I think that for the time being we've just about finished here," he said. "The lads have interviewed all the staff and guests. Can't get any sense out of Lady Pelham though. We're going to have to come back."

The other officer nodded.

"Does anybody know where Sir William is? He seems to have gone walkabout."

"No, no idea. But I've got his mobile number. I'll give him a ring in a minute. He needs to get back here before Lady Pelham goes into complete meltdown."

"Did you get anything from the guests?"

The officer grinned.

"No. Most of them just want to know when they can go home. From the panic-stricken faces of one or two of them, I suspect that some people may be here under false pretences, if you get my drift."

"Ah, the dirty weekend. Never goes out of fashion, does it? Well, if they need to get going they'd better be quick. It's only a matter of time before the press turns up. In fact, I'm surprised that they're not here already."

Aubrey and Vincent watched as the officers made their way towards the waiting police cars. The receptionist blew her nose again and sat staring into space. Aubrey turned to Vincent.

"Shall we?"

Together the two of them slipped back through the front door and ran round the side of the house towards the terrace. Sitting with their heads together were three people.

"Does anybody know where Bridie is?" asked Emily.

Jacob shrugged.

"Up in her room still weeping and wailing, I think. Making herself the centre of attention, as usual." He ran his hands through his hair and stared down at the wooden decking beneath their feet. "God, this is all we need." He looked up again. "What did the police ask you anyway?"

"Well, as soon as they knew that I was a Pelham they were much more interested," replied Emily. "I had to explain that I didn't live here, I'm only staying here. They asked me what my relationship with Guido was. I told them that I didn't have one. That as far as I knew he was an employee of my father's and that was it."

"They asked me if I'd noticed any strangers hanging about the place," said Jacob. "I was forced to point out that this is a hotel. The place is full of bloody strangers."

Edward tipped back in his chair and stared for a moment at the serene blueness of the sky. His brother and sister's voices sounded far away. He watched as the great white clouds billowed up, the huge cotton wool puffs forming and re-forming as they drifted by. There was, he thought, something very soothing about clouds. He could stare at them for hours, and sometimes as a boy he had. One of his earliest memories was that of walking with his mother, on a day very much like today, while they discussed the shapes in the sky. Later they had sat down to a picnic of egg salad sandwiches and crisps in the copse and his mother had produced a little sketch book and crayons from her straw bag. He could remember clearly how carefully he had coloured in the blue of the sky and the green of the trees and how his mother had smiled and written his name and the date on the finished picture. He wondered where it was now. Possibly his mother still had it. She had, he knew, kept many things of theirs over the years, including their school ties and handmade birthday cards as well as the photograph albums. He must ask her the next time he saw her. But where had Emily and Jacob been that day? Perhaps it was before Emily was born and after Jacob had started school. That brief heavenly period when he had his mother all to himself.

He turned to look at his brother and sister and pulled his thoughts back to the present. His own police interview had been all right, he supposed. It was difficult to tell, he hadn't ever had one to compare it with. His only experience of the police had been when he was about thirteen and he and two other boys had been racing their bikes through the village, much to the annoyance of the residents. The police officer who had spoken to them then had been kindly and avuncular and had advised them to cycle off home before he was forced to do what he called nick them. What he was going to nick them for, he hadn't said but there had been no real threat behind his words.

The two officers that had questioned him this morning had been from an entirely different school of policing. There was nothing avuncular about those two. It had been like something that you'd see in a television series, them sitting opposite him, notebooks poised, faces impassive. They hadn't been stern but they hadn't been friendly either. They had asked all the questions that he had expected, and one or two that he hadn't, carefully noting down his answers and giving the occasional nod. He hadn't been able to tell them much anyway. No, he didn't really know Guido, he was just a member of staff. No, he couldn't remember when he'd last seen him. He'd confirmed that last night he had gone up to bed fairly early. Alone. No, there wasn't anybody that could vouch for that. No, he hadn't got up in the night at all and no he hadn't heard any kind of disturbance.

As with Emily, they had asked what his relationship with Guido had been. Like Emily, he had also told them that he didn't have one, that he barely knew the man. Finally they had asked him the purpose of his visit to Seton Manor, at which point he had felt the dangerous flicker of a bubble of laughter. He could just imagine the looks on their faces if he told them that while ostensibly he had turned up to celebrate his father's birthday, in actual fact he was hoping to tap the old man for a few hundred thousand to cover his thefts at the office and thereby spare himself the experience of a spell of detention at the Her Majesty's pleasure.

The officers had requested that, as a member of the Pelham family, he didn't leave the premises for the time being and he guessed that they had said the same to Emily and Jacob. He didn't care. In fact, in a strange way he rather welcomed it. All that waited at home for him was an empty house and more sleepless nights going round and round in circles, endlessly worrying about how to repay the money he had stolen. For a while he had toyed with the idea of taking out various loans and thereby keeping his acts of theft secret but the interest rate on the kind of loans that he wanted, that is, those where the cash was ready and the questions few, were practically extortionate and how then would he repay them? He didn't have enough to maintain their lifestyle as it was. Which was how he had come to steal the money in the first place.

Jacob hadn't been wrong, he knew, when he'd pointed out Delia's extravagances. As a family they had been living beyond their means for years and to a great extent he had only himself to blame for that. He had never denied Delia anything and therefore it had never occurred to her to question their income. He was a successful solicitor, a partner in the firm, and she had simply taken for granted that the twins would go to decent schools, that she would have expensive gym membership and designer clothes, and that they would always have a gardener and a cleaner. He hadn't quite promised her that when they married but in his heart he knew that it had been implied. A couple of weeks ago he had considered the prospect of re-mortgaging the house but he couldn't do that without Delia knowing, even supposing that he could raise a mortgage large enough. He could, he knew, forge her signature but that would just add to his list of crimes and if it was discovered…

Lurching forward again, he pinned his elbows to the table and rubbed at his temples.

"Do you think that father told them about Orlando?" asked Emily.

"Nobody's mentioned it," said Jacob. "So I guess not."

The siblings looked at each other, their eyes wary. For a moment they fell silent.

"Do you think that he's going to pay?" asked Emily at last.

Edward looked up and thought for a moment.

"Well, if he hasn't told the police it rather looks like he is."

All three of them turned as Bridie stepped out on to the terrace.

CHAPTER TWENTY-FOUR

SHE REGARDED THEM in silence, her eyes sore from weeping. She had, thought Jacob, remarkably small eyes. Funny, but he'd never noticed it before. Probably because they were usually loaded down with mascara. Walking towards them she pulled back a fourth chair from the table and sat down, eyeing them suspiciously.

"What are you three doing?" she asked eventually.

"Playing hopscotch," said Jacob, his eyes hard. Without their father being present he saw no need to pretend that he liked the woman.

"Very funny," said Bridie. "There's been a death at the manor and my baby boy is missing and you three just sit around drinking."

"Mineral water, actually," said Emily. They were hardly ever on their own with Bridie, at least not if they could avoid it but, like Jacob, on the rare occasion that they were, she saw no reason to keep up the pretence. "Anyway, why are you so upset about Guido? He was only the handyman."

Even as she said it she was aware of how privileged, how callous, she sounded. But there was something about Bridie that always brought out the worst in her.

"Yes," said Edward. "what are you so bothered about?"

Bridie narrowed her eyes, making them look even smaller, and tightened her mouth.

"God, you three have got hearts of stone." She spat the words out in a flash of anger. "A man has died, another human being, and all you can say is why am I so bothered? Hard as nails, all three of you. Like your mother."

Edward jumped up suddenly and glared down at her.

"Don't you bring our mother in to this, you bloody little bitch."

Bridie smirked and leaned back.

"Your father thinks that she's brought herself into it."

"What's that supposed to mean? What are you trying to suggest?" asked Jacob, his voice cool but his eyes hard. "What has our mother got to do with Guido?"

"Not Guido. Orlando. He's over at her cottage now. Searching for him," she added triumphantly.

Edward leaned towards her, his face scarlet, and she drew back, scraping the chair legs against the wooden boards of the terrace.

"What's going on here?"

Sir William marched across the decking and looked down at them. Edward turned and glared up at him.

"Is it true that you've been over at mother's cottage, searching for Orlando?"

Sir William pulled a chair across from another table and sat down. Reaching across he clasped Bridie's hand. He held it gently in his own, as though he had captured a tiny bird.

"Please sit down and calm yourself, Edward. You have a distinct tendency to become hysterical. We must all face the fact that your mother has become slightly unhinged." He pulled a sad face, the corners of his mouth gently dropping down. "Sadly, this does sometimes happen to women of a certain age."

Next to him Bridie smirked and nodded in agreement, tossing her head slightly, as though to emphasise the luxuriousness of her thick hair which she had tied back with a pink gingham ribbon in a girlishly swishy pony tail. Sir William looked at her adoringly for a moment and then continued.

"If that is the case, and I rather suspect that it might be, your mother is to be pitied rather than condemned. However, I feared that she might have taken Orlando as some sort of act of revenge. I needed to make sure that she wasn't keeping the boy over there against his will."

"Well?" Edward thrust his chin out. "Did you find him?"

Sir William shook his head.

"No, I did not."

Emily stared at him. Unhinged? Her mother wasn't unhinged. She was a sad, lonely woman who sought solace in a gin bottle and who had been deserted by her husband and many of her friends, but she wasn't unhinged.

"However," continued Sir William, "there is another matter that has been brought to my attention." He paused and looked gravely at his three children. "At least two of you were overheard talking in the Parsley suite about the kidnap. I'm afraid that I find myself in the distressing position of having to ask you if you know anything about the abduction."

Jacob regarded him coolly. He suddenly realised how old his father was. All his life his father had been a towering figure, a commanding presence, but now, sitting next to his wife who was more than thirty years his junior he just looked old and tired. He looked, he thought, slightly pathetic.

"And why should you think that we know anything about it?" demanded Edward.

Sir William gave a wry smile.

"There is the small matter of two million pounds. I do not flatter myself," he continued, "that you visit me out of any sense of real affection. Although, God knows, Bridie and I have tried to make you welcome…"

He turned suddenly at the sound of a commotion down on the lawn. Below them stood a small group of reporters, cameras and microphones at the ready. The one at the front raised his face towards them.

"Sir William, Sir William, can you just tell us what happened? Is it true that there's been a murder at the Manor? Can you tell us who it is? Can you give us a quote?"

Sir William blinked and strode towards the edge of the terrace.

"Get off my bloody land," he roared. "Or I'll set the dogs on you."

He blinked as the cameras flashed and the little group surged forward.

"Oh great," said Jacob. "That's going to look good in the press tomorrow."

CHAPTER TWENTY-FIVE

ELIZABETH HAD RAISED her head expectantly as Sir William stamped back down the stairs and out through the front door, expecting him to say something before he left, even if it was just an apology for disturbing her. In any event, he could, she thought, at least have said goodbye. She glanced at the small carriage clock on the mantlepiece and smiled slightly. It had been her grandmother's and had survived two world wars and various house removals and yet it still remained in excellent working order. It was one of the few things that she had removed from Seton Manor when she came to the cottage. She would probably leave it to Emily when she died, she didn't think that the boys would have much use for it.

At the thought of Emily her heart grew heavier. The girl never seemed able to settle down with anybody. When she was Emily's age she was married with three children. But then, she reflected, where had that got her in the end? A lonely existence in a home that didn't even belong to her. Maybe Emily had got it right. She stood up and poured herself another gin. She might as well, there was nothing else to do and it made the time pass more quickly. Somebody had once said that a person is never bored when they're drunk, and frankly she thought that they had a point.

She had sat motionless while William searched the cottage, listening to him opening wardrobe doors and calling Orlando's name. It hadn't taken long, the cottage wasn't big and there were no outbuildings to search. And then he had just left, slamming the door behind him and striding off down the lane without so much as what her mother used to call 'a by your leave'. There had been a time, she thought, when William had told her that he couldn't bear to be away from her, that every minute without her was a lifetime, and that she was the most beautiful girl that he had ever seen. He had sworn that he would climb mountains and swim oceans for her, and she had believed him. That had been before he had started to make real money. When they had been contented in their little house in the village, with its tiny gardens front and back and even tinier kitchen and bathroom. They had bought it with a mortgage which, at the time, had seemed the most enormous debt but they had loved their life there. The house was still standing, untouched by any attempt at modernisation. She used to walk past it sometimes, just to see if any of the shrubs and flowers that she had planted in the little front garden had still survived but the last time she had strolled by she had seen a young woman with a baby standing by an open downstairs window and she had struggled to get home before bursting into tears. That woman could have been her with Jacob, forty years ago.

She wondered sometimes what might have happened if William hadn't started his own building business and been so successful? If he hadn't made the transition from being a small-time local builder to a full-blown property developer? Would they have just stayed in the little house and watched their children grow up? Marked the anniversaries with dinner at the local hotel and quietly grown old together? Even as she thought it, she knew that it would never have ended like that. William was always far too ambitious. Part of her attraction for him, she realised later, was that she was a cut above the village girls. As the daughter of a local magistrate and prosperous brewer who was prominent in local county life, she was what used to be called a catch. All right, it wasn't exactly high society, but it was higher than William's.

William's family were what people nowadays called artisan. His father had been a carpenter, a small bombastic man with a fat stomach and an aggressively bristling moustache, who ran his own carpentry business in the nearby town, and employed three men. His mother had been the company's administrator, in between being a wife and a mother to their only child, and she knew her place. Which was generally behind her husband. They had been thrilled when William had started courting her, and even more thrilled when she and William had married. Her own parents rather less so.

Looking back now, it was obvious that things had really begun to change when William had bought Seton Manor. Teetering on the brink of dereliction, the house had definitely seen better days. Standing on the edge of the village in its own grounds, it had been a number of years since it had been lived in. The last occupants had been two unmarried sisters who had inherited the property from their father and had lived on there after his death. Unfortunately, they hadn't inherited sufficient money to maintain it and so had existed in a kind of genteel poverty, keeping up appearances as best they could and growing their own vegetables. After they had died, within months of each other, the house had stood empty and neglected, gradually falling into even more disrepair.

Along with the other village children, Elizabeth had played among the trees when she was a child and occasionally, daringly, entered the empty house via a broken window at the back, tiptoeing around and hardly daring to breathe. She had always been struck by the faded grandeur of the place. The peeling paint and the once rich wallpaper hanging down in forlorn strips made her think of old movies filmed in the nineteen thirties where the heroine would sweep down a wide staircase, her little slippered feet just peeping below her great billowing Victorian gown as the man of her dreams waited for her. It made her think of fairy stories, too. The stories that her mother had read to her as a child. The whole house carried an air of lost romance. She wouldn't have been surprised to find a sleeping princess on one of the beds.

Buying Seton Manor had been Williams's dream. When they were courting they had taken picnics to eat in the overgrown orchard and over the cheese and tomato sandwiches, slices of pork pie and flasks of tea, he would talk of what he would do with the place if he ever had the money. It made her feel sad to think of those picnics now. A time of innocence, they were more than content with their tea and sandwiches. They wouldn't have dreamed of taking a bottle of wine with them. Wine had been for special occasions only and nobody drank it at home. Less easily available than now, it wasn't obtainable in the village which boasted only a general grocery shop. The nearest off-licence was about fifteen miles away. If you wanted a drink, you went to the pub. But be that as it may, William hadn't had to wait too long before his dream became a reality. Two or three really lucrative building contracts and he was on his way.

The extensive renovations that were necessary and which had put so many potential purchasers off were, of course, nothing to a builder. He had made a cash offer, somehow squared everything with the local planning department, and put a team of his own men in with the promise of large bonuses. Within a very short space of time, the twelve bedroomed Seton Manor had been restored to its former glory, with the added comforts of twentieth century living. His parents had revelled in the knowledge that their son was living in such a grand style and, truth to tell, her own parents hadn't been displeased. But that had been nothing compared to William's knighthood. If you believed his father, his son had been practically elevated to royalty.

Elizabeth smiled to herself as she sipped at her gin. How hard William had worked for that honour. How many charities he had supported. How many thousands he had donated to the local party. How hard he had tried to make the right connections. But it had paid off eventually. He had received the call and she honestly believed that it had been the proudest achievement of his life. The successful establishment of his business, the birth of his three children, were as nothing compared to that. But if things had changed when they moved into Seton Manor, they had changed even more after he became Sir William. The slightly arrogant tilt to the head, the confident way of walking, became even more pronounced. His way of speaking changed, too. The slight burr of the village accent disappeared and was replaced by the measured phrases and extended vocabulary of the men that he was now mixing with. He could almost be mistaken for the real thing.

She could sense, too, that he had begun to regard her in a different light. He no longer told her that she was beautiful and took her out for dinner in expensive restaurants, or brought her home unexpected little gifts. His business trips became more frequent and seemed always to necessitate staying away for at least one, more often two, nights. The cosy evening chats when he would pour them both a glass of sherry and tell her of his doings of the day, his successes and sometimes his failures too, became a thing of the past, and he no longer asked her opinion on anything. Sometimes he barely seemed to notice that she was in the room.

She remembered with hideous clarity the day that she had discovered what she thought was probably his first infidelity. It had been such a cliché that it was almost amusing. Sorting through his suits for the dry cleaners, she had emptied the pockets. And found a small black nylon thong edged with tiny scraps of lace. She had pulled it out and stared at it for a moment, not quite sure what she was looking at. The slow realisation had hit her like a punch in the back, a great dull thud that made her mouth dry and her heart beat faster. There was, she knew, no reasonable explanation that she could find for such a garment being in her husband's pocket.

That night she had slept in a spare room, pleading a headache, and cried herself to sleep. It would be no good, she knew, to confront him. He would simply deny it or, even worse, admit it. The challenge would then be for her to do something about it. But what? She hadn't worked outside the home for years and she had the children to consider. Besides which, she loved him. In the end she had said nothing but simply accepted it. It had been all right. They had found their own way of being and had even, she believed, been reasonably contented. When he went away on his so-called business trips she had started drinking to dull the pain and one way or another they had got through. Until Bridie, that is. Everything always came back to Bridie.

Standing up, Elizabeth drained her glass. In spite of her assumed indifference to William's clear disapproval of her way of living, she felt secretly ashamed. Sometimes she was even glad that most of her friends had deserted her. She wouldn't want any of them to see her now. There had been a time when she had chaired charity fund-raising committees and been on first name terms with the vicar. Now she had become the kind of person other people avoided, drawing their children close to them and averting their gaze. She was well aware that the cottage was the only house in the neighbourhood where the children didn't trick or treat. She didn't blame them. She was hardly an appetising sight. They probably thought that she was a witch.

On some days she didn't even bother to get showered but simply sat around in her nightdress and dressing gown, only very vaguely aware of what day it was, and watched television. Well, as she had frequently told the children when they were little, if you don't like something then do something about it. She would start right now. It was a beautiful day. She would brush her hair, put a little make up on and take a walk in the fresh air instead of sitting on her own, thinking and drinking. But first she must remember to take her pills. She had been very lax lately. It was ironic, she thought, that she needed to take pills for her heart, given that her heart had been broken. She fumbled around in the cupboard, searching for the little bottle. She was sure that she had put them in there last time. Ah well, never mind. She would take them later.

AS SHE STEPPED into the copse, the air felt fresh and cool in among the trees and she raised her face towards the sky. A feeling of euphoria swept through her and then the ground rushed up to meet her as the breath rushed from her body and a great pain cracked through her side.

CHAPTER TWENTY-SIX

JEREMY GLANCED SIDEWAYS at Carlos. Poor lad. He looked so woebegone. He had barely said a word this morning, not even to the cats who had stuck to him like little shadows in a show of support.

"Cheer up, Carlos. It's lovely to be out of doors on a morning like this and you'll soon see them again."

He said 'them' out of tact. While Carlos liked Casper very much, it was Teddy that had his heart and, thank goodness, it appeared to be reciprocated. The little scene when their father had arrived to pick them up would have been almost comical if it hadn't been quite so heart-wrenching. Carlos had stood, mute with misery, unable to speak, while Teddy's pretty little heart-shaped face was held in fierce concentration as she tried not to cry. Even Casper was quieter than usual and had obeyed his father's instruction to help him load the car without complaining.

Carlos nodded and kept his eyes on the ground as he plodded along beside him. Jeremy felt a great surge of sympathy for him. It was all very well for adults to trivialise it but teenage love was really quite like no other. It hit unsuspecting adolescents with all the force of an oncoming train and nothing could prepare them for it. One minute boys and girls were playing separate games in the playground and completely failing to see the point of the other's existence, and the next they were gawping like moon-struck calves at the object of their affection. He had been no different with his own first love. He had been aged about fourteen and had already started to notice girls as something other than an annoying nuisance who didn't even play football, and he had spotted her out of a classroom window as she was on her way towards the hockey pitch with her class mates. Small and fair, not unlike Molly now he thought about it, the image of her swinging her hockey stick, her fair hair tied neatly back and her little grey hockey skirt just reaching mid-thigh had filled his every waking minute and he had hung around school corridors and made himself late for lessons so that he could accidentally bump into her at break times.

Occasionally he had even got on the same after-school bus as her, although they lived in opposite directions. Knowing that having spent his bus money he would have to walk back just added to his sense of devotion. He had tried to sit just behind her whenever he could so that he could spend the whole journey staring at her and listen to her chattering to her friends. The day when one of his friends casually mentioned that she was dating a school prefect he had felt that his world would collapse. Prefects were practically demi-gods in his school. Usually chosen for their sporting prowess or academic excellence, how could he compete with one of those? Especially as he was only fourteen and had yet to develop the manly chest and coat hanger shoulders that all his friends said girls liked. He still squirmed when he recalled how he had lain on his stomach on his bedroom floor, listening to love songs and writing poems for her, none of which he had ever actually sent. Thank God.

He glanced across at Carlos again and then raised his head and listened to the pure clarity of the bird song. These days he rarely, if ever, stopped to listen. He always seemed to be going somewhere, doing something, too distracted to notice his surroundings. When he was a boy he had noticed everything, taking real pleasure in absorbing the sights and sounds of the world around him. He and his friends had often roamed the fields and river bank near where they lived, making camps and pretending to go hunting, and he had pretty much been able to identify each bird by its call. It was helped by the fact that the headmaster at his primary school had always played a recording of bird song at the end of every daily assembly, carefully placing the long playing record on the turntable and turning up the volume. He felt suddenly sad. Most schools these days probably didn't even have regular assemblies, let alone a rotund little head master playing bird song to set his pupils up for the day.

He breathed in deeply and let his shoulders relax. There might not be bird song played in school assemblies these days but life was good. The sun was climbing high in the sky but there was a light breeze that just brushed against his face. Molly, with her usual empathy, had suggested that he and Carlos go for a short walk while she got on with the packing and he had immediately agreed. With a slightly worrying echo of his father, he had remarked with a forced air of jollity that a bit of fresh air would do them both good. Next to him Carlos continued to mooch along in silence, his hands in his pockets and his eyes still on the ground. Ah well, no doubt he'd talk when he wanted to. Anyway, sometimes silence was good.

When he was teaching at Sir Frank's, one of the things that had always annoyed him was the insistence by the head, who didn't actually do any teaching herself, that all pupils must participate, by which she meant contribute verbally. Well, what if they didn't want to? What if they were perfectly happy just sitting there and absorbing? Not everybody wanted to talk. Some children were more reserved than others, and why shouldn't they be? But there was no point in trying to reason with the head. As far as she was concerned, there were two ways of doing things –

her way and the wrong way. Suffice to say that in the end he had just smiled and nodded along with everybody else and then tried to meet his students needs in his own way. It seemed to have worked, for the most part. At least his classes didn't regularly riot or slash his tyres. At Sir Frank's, that was a mark of acceptance.

Head slightly to one side as he listened to the birds, he started to plan the journey home. There was a petrol station in the nearby town so he could fill up there and if the traffic was okay and they avoided the motorways and the risk of tailbacks, then with luck they should be back home within a few hours. At the thought of home his spirits lifted. He'd enjoyed their holiday, what little they'd had of it, but given the choice he always preferred to be at home. They could have a take-away tonight and maybe watch a film. Carlos would like that, it might cheer him up a bit. The cats would like it, too. They always ordered more than they could eat which meant that Aubrey and Vincent could hoover up the leftovers.

Marching slightly ahead of them, Aubrey and Vincent led the way. Jeremy had wanted to put them in their baskets ready for the journey home, knowing only too well the magic disappearing act that cats did whenever they were needed to be somewhere, but Aubrey and Vincent had taken evasive action by simply jumping off the balcony. Jeremy looked at them and smiled fondly. They were a good looking pair.

Aubrey turned to Vincent.

"Looks like we're going home this morning."

Vincent nodded. They could hardly have failed to spot the cat baskets being brought up from the car.

"Be quite nice to get back," he said. "See what's been happening. Sort of makes you appreciate it more, if you see what I mean."

Aubrey did see what he meant. While just being with Molly and Jeremy was about as good as it could get, there were lots of things about their manor that they thoroughly enjoyed. Annoying next door's dog just being one of them. He grinned. Poor old Beryl. They were very fond of her really but she fell for it every time, barking and yelping as Vincent sat just out of reach, swinging his tail and washing his ears.

They paused and waited for Jeremy and Carlos to catch up.

"What do you think that Sir William is going to do about that boy?" asked Carlos, breaking his silence at last.

Jeremy shrugged, his expression worried.

"I don't really know. My instinct is that we should tell the police but he was insistent that we didn't." He paused and then continued. "I suppose I sort of understand it in a way. I mean imagine if somebody took one of the cats?"

They both stopped, appalled at the mere thought. Vincent turned to Aubrey.

"I knew a cat that got catnapped once."

"Did you?" Aubrey asked, fascinated. "What happened."

"It was one of those posh ones. It was called Gilbert and it had this diamond collar. Anyway, one night the house that Gilbert lived in got burgled."

"What? And they took him?"

"Amongst other things. And then his owners got a note asking for money. I used to live next door to them," he added casually.

Aubrey nodded. Vincent had, he knew, lived with an elderly lady at one time. In a moment of weakness he had once confided in Aubrey that she had named him Mr Fluffypot, a fact to which he had never referred again. And Aubrey didn't blame him. He wouldn't either. One of the tough things about being owned was that you didn't get to choose your own name. In fact some names were so embarrassing that he had known cats lie about it. Bruce had almost got away with it until some of the cats on the manor overheard his owners calling for Piddly over the garden fence.

"What happened to Gilbert?" Aubrey asked. "Did they pay."

Vincent narrowed his eyes.

"Yes, but they didn't send Gilbert back. He was found two months later."

Aubrey held his breath.

"Dead," continued Vincent.

"What, did he have a heart attack or something?" said Aubrey hopefully.

"Don't ask. Anyway, his owners moved away soon after. They said that they couldn't stand living there anymore."

They both fell silent.

"When we lived in Brazil," said Carlos, unaware of the serious conversation that had just taken place by his feet, "there was this kidnapping. It was some rich bloke's wife, and somebody told the police."

"Did they? What happened?"

"They never found her."

"Did they catch the kidnappers?"

Carlos shook his head.

"No. Some people said that she was taken out to sea and fed to the sharks."

"I don't think that's very likely here, Carlos."

Carlos looked thoughtful.

"No, I suppose not. I don't think there's any sharks to start with. Why not?"

"Why not what?"

"Why aren't there any sharks here? It's not that far from the sea. I mean, how do sharks decide where to live? I mean, like, do they just stay where they're born or do they move around?"

Jeremy suppressed a grin. Carlos was obviously starting to feel a little better.

"I don't know. We'll look it up when we get home. But wherever the boy is, whoever's got him, must have planned it," said Jeremy. "I mean, surely it can't have been an opportunistic thing."

"An oppo what?"

"Opportunistic. It means suddenly seeing a chance and taking it. Like somebody breaking into a house because they see a window open." He thought for a moment. "If you think about it logically, whoever's got Orlando must have been prepared. I mean you can't just rush off into the night with a kid stuffed under your arm and no idea where you're going to take him. And it would have to be somewhere where nobody would see him and that he couldn't escape from."

"Somewhere with a lock and without windows?" suggested Carlos.

"Maybe." Jeremy nodded. "Something like that, anyway. And I can't help thinking that he must have been taken by somebody that he knew. I mean, from the little that I saw of him he didn't look like the kind of child that would do something that he didn't want to. In fact, quite the opposite." He paused. "You know that Sir William told Molly and me that the Parsley suite is occupied by his son Jacob?"

Carlos stared.

"What, you mean he's kidnapped his own brother?"

"I don't know. I guess that it's a possibility. My feeling is that there's no love lost between the second Lady Pelham and the three older children. But whoever's got him, somebody needs to find him soon, that's for sure."

Aubrey agreed. After leaving the hotel this morning he and Vincent had searched every place that they could think of where a boy might be hiding. They had even checked out the old pig sty. They had found nothing. Not a trace. Wherever he was, he was nowhere within the grounds of the manor. But, reflected Aubrey, at least they had done what they had said they would do. They had searched, and they had searched thoroughly. They had nothing to recriminate themselves with. He walked on a little into the cool relief of the shade of the copse and flopped down on the flattened grass where Teddy and Casper's camp had been. Rolling over onto his back he glimpsed something sticking out from behind a tree. He screwed up his eyes and looked harder. It looked like a shoe. Must have been left by Teddy and Casper. But it didn't look like any sort of shoe that either of them would have worn, they both wore trainers. It looked more like one of Molly's shoes, but Molly hadn't been over here. Curious now, he sat up and wandered over to it. He was right, it was a shoe. But this shoe had a leg attached to it.

CHAPTER TWENTY-SEVEN

MOLLY GLANCED UP from the case that she was fastening as Jeremy and Carlos came in. Jeremy sat down heavily on the sofa. Carlos flopped down next to him, his expression glum.

"I'd take your time with that Moll, if I were you."

Molly straightened up and looked from one to the other.

"Why, what's happened?"

"Well, I don't think that we'll be going home just yet." He paused for a moment and swallowed before speaking. There wasn't really a gentle way to put this. "Another body has been found."

Molly took a deep breath.

"Who?" she said at last. "Not the little boy? Not Orlando?"

Jeremy shook his head.

"No. Not Orlando."

"Who then?"

"The first Lady Pelham."

Molly sat down in the small armchair and ran her hand through her hair.

"What happened? I mean, was she…"

"I don't know. There was no obvious sign of injury."

"Who found her? Was it you?"

"Yes, or more accurately, Aubrey. He was fussing around by one of the trees and making that dreadful yowling noise he does when he wants some attention. At first I thought that he'd injured himself."

"It was horrible." Carlos spoke for the first time and then fell silent again. It was true. It was horrible. Not just finding the body, which was bad enough, but finding it where they had done. The copse had been such a happy place when he had been with Teddy and Casper. The memories which he had carefully stored of sitting with them by the candles and stuffing their faces with chocolate, watching Teddy's animated face and breathing in the scent of her hair, were spoiled. Now somebody had met their death there and it felt like the sun had slipped behind a permanent shadow.

"Try not to dwell on it, Carlos," Jeremy said. He resisted the temptation to say that it could have been much worse although, in fact, it could. At least Elizabeth Pelham had looked peaceful, just as though she were asleep really.

"We went over to where Aubrey was," Carlos continued. "And she was laying on her side and just sort of staring straight ahead. Her skirt was pulled up a bit."

Molly looked horrified, her small face twisted.

"You don't mean…"

Jeremy jumped up and put his arm round her.

"No, I don't think so. I think that perhaps she took a tumble and her skirt got caught up as she fell."

Molly's shoulders relaxed slightly.

"Thank Goodness for that. How do you think that she died?"

Jeremy frowned.

"No idea. As I said, there was no obvious sign of injury. No blood or anything She was just lying there. I thought at first that she was drunk so I leaned over and tugged slightly on her arm. I thought that we'd better get her home rather than just leave her there. But there was no response and when I looked more closely, I could just see it. I just knew that she was dead." He thought for a moment. "To say that there's an absence of life sounds trite, but that's what it was. An absence of life."

Aubrey had known that she was dead, too. In fact he had known straight away, which was why he had made such a fuss to get attention. Over the years he had developed that ear-splitting yowl to perfection and it always got results.

"Luckily," Jeremy continued, "Carlos had his mobile with him."

Not lucky at all, thought Aubrey. There was never an occasion when Carlos didn't have his mobile with him. Even at night he laid it carefully on his bedside table and made sure that it was within easy reach. Carlos's mobile was as much a part of him as his right arm. Unlike Jeremy, who frequently left his at home or forgot to put it on to charge.

"Did you ring the police?" asked Molly.

"Of course. And then we waited with the body until they turned up."

"What did they say when they arrived?"

"It was the same officer. The one that came to the apartment." Jeremy grinned suddenly. "He said, you seem to be making a bit of a habit of this sir, you and the lad. And I had to agree with him. Anyway, somebody's coming over later to take our statements so we can't go just yet."

"I'll stick this lot back in our bedroom," said Molly, pulling one of the cases towards her. "I hope that the police won't keep us for too long. I'd rather like to get home now. Carlos, stick the kettle on. We might as well have a coffee while we're waiting."

She watched for a moment as Carlos trailed into the kitchen, followed by Aubrey and Vincent. Frankly, the sooner they got home and back to normality, the better. In her opinion, two dead bodies turning up was two too many.

CHAPTER TWENTY-EIGHT

EMILY RAISED HER head, her eyes red from weeping, and ran her fingers through her hair. She ought to make herself look respectable and go downstairs again. When her father had broken the news to them, in that spare matter of fact way he used when faced with something distasteful, she had stared at him, unable to speak, and then rushed out. Where Jacob and Edward had gone or what they had said, she had no idea. She had heard a great rushing sound in her ears as though she might faint and then she had simply fled to the safety of her room and locked the door behind her. She dipped her head as she felt her throat thicken and her eyes fill again.

Poor Mummy. Poor, poor Mummy. Her life hadn't been much fun since the advent of Bridie but she would have pulled it round again. She just knew that she would. Maybe even, with time, have met somebody else. Older people did, all the time. Especially now that there was all this on-line stuff available. A friend's mother had paired up with somebody and re-married at the age of seventy-five. And mummy was still attractive, when she made the effort. The next time she saw her, she thought, she'd show her how to use one of the dating sites. Get her registered on one, make her get her hair done and take some decent photographs of her and… only she couldn't. She wasn't going to see Mummy again.

She thought with a sudden hot bubbling of guilt of the last time she had seen her mother, staggering around drunk at that dreadful birthday reception for Daddy. She or Edward or Jacob should have gone home with her, they should have done more, they should have…

She turned at the sound of a light rapping. Jacob put his head around the door.

"Can I come in, Em?"

Emily nodded and gestured towards one of the little chairs. Jacob sat down and regarded her.

"You look a right wreck, Em."

"Thank you so much, Jacob. You are, of course, a thing of beauty. As always."

They smiled suddenly at each other and Jacob pulled a small bottle from his pocket.

"Thought you could do with this."

He unscrewed the half bottle of brandy and passed it to her. Rising, she fetched two tooth glasses from the bathroom and poured them each a large measure.

"Cheers."

"Cheers," replied Jacob.

"Where's Ed?"

Jacob shrugged his shoulders.

"He said that he was going for a walk. I asked him if he wanted some company and he said no so I left him to it. I rang the police though. Thought I'd see if I could get any more information out of them, I mean, Father didn't exactly large it on the detail." He sighed. "I just felt like I needed to be doing something rather than just sitting around."

"What did they say?"

"Not much more than Father told us. She was found over in the copse by that family staying in one of the apartments, the same ones that found Guido. There was no apparent injury and no obvious cause of death."

"Will there be an autopsy?"

Jacob frowned.

"Bound to be. Unexpected death."

"Was it? Unexpected, I mean?" asked Emily.

"As far as I know. I mean, we know that she had problems with her heart but she was taking medication for that and I don't think it had got any worse." He paused. "Of course, she did drink too much."

Emily nodded and sipped slowly at her brandy, feeling the reviving warmth seep through her.

"It seems unbelievable. I mean, I can't quite take it in. She's not here anymore…"

Jacob agreed. It did seem unbelievable. Their mother had been an absolute constant in their lives and even now, in his forties, she was the person that he would always turn to if he was troubled about anything. In fact he had planned to visit her in the cottage later that day to discuss the redundancy situation with her. She didn't have any money of her own to help him out but just sharing the problem with her would have been a comfort. She would have found something sensible to say, something reassuring. And now she was gone. Forever.

"Do you think that Daddy actually cares?" asked Emily. "I mean, he didn't look like he did. For God's sake, how long were they married? You'd think that he might have shown some emotion."

Jacob leaned back in his chair and shook his head regretfully.

"All he cares about now is Bridie and Orlando. Everyone else can go to hell as far as he's concerned. Mother was just something that was hanging around from the past. Like us," he added. "My guess is that he was more upset about Guido, it means that he's got to go to the trouble of finding a new handyman. If he feels anything about Mother it's probably annoyance that the few remaining guests will almost certainly leave now. And I doubt that they'll pay their bills."

"Where is he now?"

"On the terrace, with Bridie. It's a bit stuffy in here, Em. Do you mind if I open a window?"

Without waiting for an answer, Jacob got up and unfastened the latch, throwing the window wide open. From the terrace below the sound of his father's voice drifted upwards. Emily and Jacob looked at each other. Emily raised an eyebrow. Wordlessly they positioned themselves within ear shot.

"Of course, there will be the funeral to arrange." Sir William's voice, loud and confident as ever, spiralled up towards them.

"Funeral?" whispered Jacob, spitting the words out in a wave of fury. "She's barely cold. We don't even know the cause of death yet. She's his ex-wife, with the emphasis on the ex. What bloody business is it of his?"

He edged closer to the open window as his father continued.

"I suppose that I should let people know, although of course she had very few friends left." Sir William sighed. "She just seemed to drive everybody away."

No, thought Emily. She didn't drive everybody away. She didn't drive us away. She peered round the window frame and regarded her father with dislike, drawing quickly back in case he spotted her. She pressed her lips together. She knew very well what he was up to. This was his opportunity to rehabilitate himself with the local community. To create his own false narrative. To be seen, publicly, doing the right thing by a wife that had been, frankly, too difficult to live with. A wife that had taken to drink and committed the cardinal female sin of, what he would call, letting herself go. As he would no doubt tell people at the wake, to which most of the village would turn up. Free drinks on Sir William didn't often happen.

"It's not really your responsibility, Billy." Bridie's voice, edged with the velvet that she always reserved for their father, was both soothing and sultry. "Honestly Billy, I don't see why you should have all the bother. I mean, she has got three grown-up children. They're her next of kin. Surely it's up to them to make the arrangements. Really, it's got nothing to do with you. I mean, it's not like you're actually related or anything."

Jacob nodded. For once, he and Bridie were in agreement.

"You are so sweet, as ever my dear. Always thinking of others. But I feel that I must do this. I doubt very much that Elizabeth put by sufficient funds."

Emily gripped her tooth glass harder. Of course mummy didn't put by sufficient funds. She barely had enough to live on.

"I'll speak to Roger at the Lodge. He owns a chain of undertakers. He can arrange for everything to be done properly. No, my dear," he continued as Bridie began to protest. "It will be much better this way. After all, she was my wife."

"A pity that he didn't remember that before," Emily turned to Jacob and whispered through gritted teeth. "Paying for her bloody funeral is the least he can do. Although," she added, "if we take care of it then we can at least ensure that Bridie doesn't come."

"Good thinking," said Jacob. "That's if we can raise the money. And," he added, "if we can elbow father out of the way. And let's be honest, Em, he takes a bit of elbowing."

For a moment there was silence from below and then Bridie's voice floated upwards again.

"Well Billy, do bear in mind the cost. It's not a state occasion." She laughed, a light trilling sound that grated on the ears of the unseen listeners. "I mean, there's no need to go mad."

"Unbelievable," said Jacob. "Bloody unbelievable. She's taken Mother's husband, her home, more or less everything that she had, and now she begrudges her a decent funeral."

He took a gulp of brandy and listened harder.

"Besides which," Bridie continued, "we have far more important matters to think about." Her voice cracked suddenly. "Oh Billy, what are we going to do?"

There was a moment's silence. No doubt, thought Emily, Daddy was putting his arm around her or patting her pretty little hand, indulging in one of those sickening displays of affection that had been noticeably absent when they were growing up but which he frequently demonstrated when Bridie was around. She moved slightly closer to the open window as Sir William continued.

"As you know my dear, the last text simply stated that the money must be paid into an account, the details of which will be provided in due course so at present there is nothing that we can do except wait." Jacob and Emily sensed rather than saw their father frown. "I was expecting something today but so far there has been nothing." Sir William paused and lowered his voice, although as far as he was aware there was nobody to hear him. "You know really my darling, I'm starting to think that we must involve the police. I hate to say this to you, but there's every possibility that the money will be paid but Orlando will not be returned. If we inform the police, at the very least they may be able to tell us where the phone signal is coming from."

Emily and Jacob moved swiftly away from the window as Bridie jumped up and pushed back her chair. She let out a loud wail.

"No, Billy! We can't! They'll hurt him. We can't involve the police."

CHAPTER TWENTY-NINE

JEREMY GLANCED DOWN at his watch. He still wore a watch even though Carlos had repeatedly told him that nobody wore them anymore. What was the point of having a watch when you had a phone? But Jeremy liked his watch. It had belonged to his grandfather and with its old-fashioned clear dial and thick leather strap, it had a solid weightiness about it that he found comforting. Somebody had once told him that it was probably worth quite a bit of money but he would never sell it. Not least because it was about the only item in the house that he didn't have to remember to put on charge.

"What time is it?" Molly asked.

"Just gone five. You know, I was thinking Moll, it's hardly worth setting off now. We might as well stay tonight and make an early start tomorrow morning."

Molly nodded.

"I was thinking the same. Perhaps later we can walk down to the village pub and have a meal there. It'll give us something to do and I've got a feeling that the hotel dining room won't be open."

"I think that you're probably right. From the empty state of the car park, it looks like most of the guests have left now."

"Do you think that the police will need us for anything else?" asked Molly.

"I shouldn't think so. Anyway, they've got our address and phone numbers."

For a moment they both fell silent again, thinking about the police officer who had only just gone. Tall and thin, with the kind of bony hands that always look cold, and wearing the sort of suit that was surely beyond the average copper's salary, he had come unsmiling into the apartment and without an introduction had simply flipped open his notebook. He had narrowed his eyes and tipped his head to one side as Jeremy described finding Elizabeth Pelham in the copse. He had looked at him in an appraising way which made Jeremy feel distinctly uncomfortable. It was not unlike the way he had felt when, as a boy, his father had questioned him over some misdemeanour, and he had to force himself to look the officer in the eye. When he had finished explaining, the police officer had said nothing for a moment but simply looked at him as though waiting for him to continue. When it became apparent that there was nothing more to be said about the finding of Elizabeth Pelham he had expressed sardonic surprise that Jeremy and Carlos had, yet again, apparently stumbled upon another corpse.

The officer's questioning as to whether they had any prior connection with the Pelham family or Seton Manor had been even more uncomfortable. He had been particularly insistent on the point, in spite of their assurances that they were only there on holiday and had never heard of the place or Sir William before. But most difficult at all had been his repeated question as to whether there was anything else that they could tell him, whether there was anything that they thought might be significant. He hadn't quite accused them of holding something back but the suggestion had hung in the air. Jeremy, keeping his gaze firmly fixed ahead of him, had been only too aware that all three of them were indeed holding something back. That something being the missing Orlando.

IN HIS ROOM, Carlos sat on his bed and waited impatiently for Teddy to answer his WhatsApp call. It was funny, he'd really liked this place when they arrived. He'd even dreamed of living somewhere like this when he was older, when he was a celebrated chef with loads of money in the bank. Now it was tainted with the stench of death and he couldn't wait to get home and away from here, back to his own familiar bedroom with the cats curled up on the end of his bed and the sound of Jeremy stomping around the house looking for his phone charger or his car keys. He leaned forward as Teddy's face suddenly appeared on the screen.

"Carlos, are you okay? What's happening?"

"There's been another body."

Teddy's eyes widened making her look, Carlos thought, even prettier. If that were possible. She pushed a strand of hair back from her face and leaned forward slightly.

"Oh no. Who is it? It's not the little boy is it? Not Sir William's son?"

Carlos shook his head and grinned suddenly as Casper's face loomed over Teddy's shoulder and filled the screen. Teddy elbowed him back out of the way.

"Go away, Casper. Go and blow yourself up or something."

Ignoring her, Casper settled himself next to her and took out a little notebook.

"So who is it?" continued Teddy.

"Sir William's first wife."

"No!" Teddy sounded genuinely shocked. "What happened?"

Carlos shrugged.

"Nobody knows yet."

"Who found her?" asked Casper, clicking the end of his pen, poised ready to take notes.

"We did," said Carlos. "Me and Jeremy. And Aubrey."

As he said it, he felt suddenly sick. A nasty feeling of nausea started to pulsate through him and he felt a prickle of sweat on his forehead. It felt like that time some of the kids in his class at Sir Frank's had been drinking strong cider and he'd thought it was a good idea to join them. To this day even the smell of cider made him feel like he wanted to throw up. He gripped his phone harder.

"Carlos, are you all right?"

Carlos nodded and swallowed, waiting for the feeling to pass. Since finding the first Lady Pelham laying in the copse the shocking memory of his own mother's death had billowed up and threatened to overwhelm him. He had deliberately turned his thoughts away from the images, making himself think of other things, refusing to let it find release, but it had fought its way out and thrust itself forward while he was talking to Teddy and he was unable to stop it. It had taken him straight back to that dreadful moment when he had discovered his mother laying on her bed, her poor bruised face turned to the wall and her lifeless eyes staring upwards. He had known then, with a dreadful finality, that with her death things had changed forever.

When his father had left, things had barely changed. If anything, life had improved. They no longer had to listen to his whisky fuelled rantings or creep about while he slept off one of his hangovers, each of which seemed to run into the next so that the clear-eyed handsome youth that Maria had married lay buried deep within the ruins of the grown man he had become. In truth, what Carlos had really felt when he left was a sense of relief, of freedom, of a new beginning. But with Maria gone the central core of his existence had started to crumble. On discovering her body he had simply run out into the night, blundering around, frightened to go back but frightened to go anywhere else. In the end, scared and cold, he had made his way towards his teacher's house and sat in his shed while he tried to think what to do.

Jeremy and Molly had never actually told him the details of the ensuing trial, brushing over the detail whenever he asked, but he could imagine it well enough. And the local papers hadn't spared any details, even though both Molly and Jeremy had tried to keep them away from him. The kids at Sir Frank's had been rather less sensitive and the news of his mother's murder had made him a minor celebrity for a short time, bringing him the kind of friends that he didn't really want.

"Carlos," Teddy sounded insistent now. "You don't look well, you've gone awfully pale. Perhaps you'd better lie down, you've had a dreadful shock. We can talk later."

Carlos nodded and laid his phone gently down on the bedside table. Swinging his legs up on to the bed he lay still and closed his eyes while he waited for the nausea to pass. The image of his mother floated gently before him and he smiled. The dreadful picture of her lying dead on her bed had gone now and been replaced by a picture of her bustling around in their apartment in Sao Paulo, her thick hair tied back with a blue ribbon, singing to herself as she flicked a duster across the shelves. He was conscious that he dreamed of her less often now and the dreams that he had were no longer nightmares but of the good times, her laughter and her singing, her sudden rushes of affection when she would clasp him to her in a great bear hug. He found himself wondering if she would have liked Teddy. On the whole he thought that she would. Turning on his side he slid gently into sleep.

CHAPTER THIRTY

AUBREY SLIPPED OFF the end of Carlos's bed. He was sleeping peacefully now so he might as well leave him to it and go and look for Vincent. Padding quietly out of the room and into the sitting room he paused for a moment and listened. Everywhere was silent. Presumably Molly and Jeremy had gone out for a walk. Leaping from the balcony he spotted Vincent staring down into the swimming pool.

"All right, Vin?"

Vincent nodded.

"I was just thinking."

Aubrey waited in silence. There was no point in rushing Vincent. He did a lot of thinking and he'd talk when he wanted to.

"That woman that we found today. If she was done in, then why leave her there?"

Aubrey felt slightly confused. Everybody had to be somewhere. Even when they were dead.

"I mean," continued Vincent. "Somebody would be bound to find her before too long."

"Perhaps that was the idea?" suggested Aubrey.

"Maybe." Vincent didn't sound convinced. "But if you ask me, she wasn't done in at all. Anyway, it looks like we're here for another night. Might as well make the most of it. Might be something doing in the kitchens if the chefs are still there."

Aubrey nodded. Making friends with the hotel chefs had been one of their priorities on arrival and so far it had proved particularly profitable. They had, as Vincent had said to Aubrey, struck gold. One of the chefs had two cats of his own and thought nothing of putting down little pieces of fillet steak or poached haddock for them to eat. And fillet steak and poached haddock was something that they never got at home, much as Molly and Jeremy loved them.

Together, the two cats strolled off across the lawn and towards the hotel. To the right of the building stood a large brick structure, the outside covered in ivy in keeping with the manor house. As they approached a car drew up and, leaning out of the window, the driver pointed a remote control at the door. Fascinated, the cats watched as the huge heavy metal door slowly swung up and over revealing a cavernous space within. Aubrey moved forward and then stopped as Vincent held him back.

"Don't go in there, Aubsie. Once that door shuts you'll never get out again."

Aubrey nodded. Vincent was right. There was something very uncompromising about that door. He sat quietly and watched as Sir William drove the car into the space and then emerged carrying a huge bunch of flowers tied with ribbons. Pointing the remote control back at the building he closed the door behind him. Aubrey looked around him. He was intrigued by the big cave like space that they had seen, maybe there was another way in and out. There usually was to most places. He glanced upwards.

"What do you think's up there?"

Vincent tipped his head to one side and screwed up his eyes. Above the triple garage was another storey with windows set high up just under the roof.

"Can't be cars," Aubrey continued. "They couldn't get them up there." He turned his head and looked across to the huge poplar tree which grew next to the garage and grinned. "Race you."

Without waiting for a response, he ran towards the tree and scrambled rapidly up the trunk, his paws easily finding holds as he climbed higher and higher. Just behind him, Vincent scaled the branches, his lithe body twisting and turning as he caught up with Aubrey and then overtook him. Reaching the top, they sat in the forked trunk and surveyed the landscape. Rolled out before them like a magnificent painting sat the English countryside in all its high summer glory. Vincent lifted his head and breathed in the scented air. Next to him Aubrey lay with his paws hanging down, relaxed. He was glad that they were going home tomorrow. It had upset him to see Carlos so obviously feeling unwell. Carlos was hardly ever ill, rarely even so much as a headache, so to see him looking so pale and wan was disturbing. He'd be better once they were back home. They all would. He turned his head to one side and found himself looking directly into the windows of the upper storey of the garage. There, on the floor, stout little legs splayed out, watching television and with one hand dipped into a giant bag of sweets, sat Orlando.

CARLOS SAT QUIETLY, with Aubrey and Vincent tucked up around his feet. Molly sat opposite him, pretending to read a magazine. She glanced upwards. He still looked pale, which was hardly surprising. He had come rushing towards them as they turned up the lane from the village and into the grounds of Seton Manor, with both cats rushing after him. At first he had been barely coherent, the words pouring out in a great babbling rush, until finally they had calmed him down and he'd told them what he had discovered. They had listened with a growing sense of alarm and then Jeremy had hastened over to Seton Manor.

"Do you feel like talking, Carlos?" Molly spoke quietly.

Carlos hunched his shoulders and gave a slight, reluctant, nod. No, he didn't really feel like talking but maybe if he told Molly then she could tell Sir William and he wouldn't have to. He didn't like Sir William. He was big and loud and he thought he owned the world, like that geography teacher with the big beard at Sir Frank's whose main method of teaching was bullying and humiliation. Jeremy had told him that it was the geography teacher's way of ensuring that nobody chose his subject in Year 10 so he had smaller classes and less work to do. It had worked a treat.

Molly laid the magazine down.

"Just start at the beginning."

Carlos remained silent for a moment and then picked Aubrey up and placed him across his lap, his long thin fingers gently running across his thick fur and keeping his head down as he spoke. Aubrey lay quietly with his paws hanging down and listened along with Molly, although he already knew the story.

"I was talking to Teddy and I didn't feel very well. I think it was, like, you know, finding…" He paused and raised his head. "I didn't feel like that when it was the handy bloke in the swimming pool. But Mrs Pelham, or whatever she's called… it sort of, you know, like, reminded me of mum and that."

Molly nodded sympathetically.

"It's hardly surprising that you should be upset. It must have been a terrible shock, both for you and Jeremy."

"So," continued Carlos, "Teddy said that I should, like, lie down. So I did."

Molly suppressed as smile. If Teddy told him to swim the English channel he'd give it his best shot. Carlos chewed on his bottom lip for a moment.

"Anyway, I must have fallen asleep because the next thing I knew was that Aubrey and Vincent were jumping on my bed and making that noise. You know."

Molly nodded. She did know. Unfortunately.

"And then what?"

"Well, I thought that they wanted me to get up so I did. I felt better by then anyway. Like, I didn't feel sick and that anymore. Then I found your note on the table that said you'd gone for a walk so I decided that I'd come and find you." He paused and thought for a moment before continuing. "When I left the apartment the cats came with me and started walking ahead, you know, like they do, with their tails in the air and they were going towards Seton Manor. And I thought that maybe they wanted to show me something so I followed them."

"And they went to the garage?" prompted Molly.

"Yes, and I thought, what's so interesting about the garage? I mean, like there's only cars and that in there. So I walked round it and noticed a little door to one side. And I tried the handle and it was open so I went in. There were stairs in front of me so I went up them. To be honest Molly, I was a bit scared. But I sort of had this feeling that I should go and look. When I got to the top there was another door and when I pushed it, that was open too."

"And that's where you found him?"

Carlos nodded.

"He was just sitting on the floor watching television. He turned round when I came in but then just turned back and carried on watching. It was some sort of detective programme or something. An old one, I think." He fell silent for a moment.

He didn't think that it was an old programme. He knew that it was. It was one in a series that his mother used to watch when they first got a television. All roads today seemed to lead back to his mother. He felt his heart lift suddenly. Maybe that was a good thing. He didn't believe in ghosts but today he had a real sense that she was with him.

"So what happened next?"

"Well, I went in and I said his name and then I said that everybody was looking for him. And then I suddenly got a bit sort of panicky and I thought, what if there's somebody else here? What if the kidnapper's in another room? So I thought that the best thing to do was to try to find you and Jeremy. Which I did. I mean," he added hastily, "Orlando wasn't hurt or anything. He was just, like I said, watching television. And eating sweets."

He placed Aubrey on the floor and stood up.

"Is it all right if I tell Teddy and Casper?"

CHAPTER THIRTY-ONE

EDWARD SAT IN the small chair set next to the fireside, one of his mother's photograph albums on his lap. He wanted to look through it but somehow he couldn't bring himself to open it. He wasn't even sure why he had come over here. It was just some sort of instinct, some need to be near his mother or at least to have a sense of her. It had galled him to have to ask his father for the key to the cottage and for several moments he'd thought that he was going to refuse but in the end it had been handed over without a word.

Outside it was growing dark. The police had left, presumably having found nothing of interest to explain his mother's death and now he was on his own. Emily and Jacob had walked down to the village pub but he hadn't wanted to go with them. He knew that the whole of the village would be talking and he didn't want to be at the centre of their curiosity. What he wanted was some peace and quiet, some time on his own to reflect. He brushed his hand across the cover of the album. His mother had loved taking photographs and, truth to tell, she hadn't been a bad photographer. All of their childhood and teenaged years were captured in these albums as well as photographs of his and Jacob's weddings.

Gently, he flicked the album open and smiled. There, right on the first page, was a photograph of the holiday that they'd had in Yarmouth. They had all agreed afterwards that it was the best holiday they'd ever had. He peered closer. That was the year they had made their most magnificent sand castle and the picture showed them building it. He felt his eyes fill as he gazed down at the image of him and Jacob filling buckets with sand, their narrow little shoulder blades jutting out and their skinny legs hanging out of their shorts. Emily in her ruched swim suit, with gaps in her teeth and a determined expression on her face, crouched down next to them as she arranged the shells that she had collected ready for decoration. That had been their last holiday in England. After that, as their father got richer and richer, the sea side holidays had stopped and they began to take holidays abroad.

Edward grimaced as the memory of those later holidays surfaced. They had, all three of them, dreaded it when their mother staggered home with that season's brochures. It seemed to them that no matter where they went, no matter how far they travelled, it was all the same place. They had hated the bustling noisy airports and the big sparkling hotels with the cheesy waiters who addressed them as sir and madam as if it was some big joke. They had hated the blazing sun that beat down on their pale English skin, and they had hated the alien food that none of them liked or even, sometimes, recognised. The swimming pools had always been far too full for them to enjoy themselves and they had often ended up in the games room, playing a resentful game of table tennis. Each day had passed drearily into the next and they had, all three of them, longed to be back home and spending the school holidays mucking about with their friends.

The thing that they had hated most of all had been the culture trips that the tour company always organised, usually to some art gallery or museum, and which their father insisted that they must go on. On those days they had trailed around in the heat and dust, longing to get into some shade, to get back into the cool of their rooms, and trying not to yawn while their guide explained the significance of a particular statue or pointed out the beauty of a particular painting. And on every holiday, without fail, there had always been a group barbecue with what the hotel described as entertainment, the entertainment usually comprising something along the lines of an Elvis impersonator and a magician. The only photographs of those holidays showed them as sulky teenagers, reluctant to pose for the camera and determined not to enjoy themselves. And then there had been no holidays at all. Jacob had gone to university and he and Emily simply weren't interested when their parents went off on cruises, opting instead to stay with their mother's sister nearby.

As he stared down at the photographs, Edward realised with a sense of surprise that he probably owned the albums now. Well, he and Em and Jacob. In fact, as next of kin, they presumably owned all of her possessions, such as they were. He glanced around and tried to work out how much of the stuff in the cottage had belonged to her and how much had already been there when she moved in. It had been previously let, he knew, as a holiday cottage. The clock on the mantlepiece had been hers, he was certain. He remembered it as a child and thought that it had belonged to his grandmother. Everything else, he wasn't so sure. There could be some jewellery that Em might like to have, but he doubted that there was much else. He wondered if she had made a will. He thought it unlikely. She'd never spoken of one, at least not to him, and given that he was the solicitor in the family he was sure that she would have at least mentioned it.

He got up from the chair and wandered over to the window. What had she done with her time here, he wondered. How had she filled her days? She had enjoyed sewing and knitting when they were younger and had taught all three of them both of those crafts, being firmly of the belief that boys as well as girls should know at least how to sew on a button, but there was no sign of her sewing box or knitting bag now. He closed his eyes as he felt his throat thicken. In his heart he knew the answer. She drank. Each day simply merged into the next with the aid of a bottle of gin. Some nights when he had telephoned her she had barely been coherent. He felt his heart ache. He should have done more, they all should. They should have stood up to their father, they should have insisted that she received a decent settlement, they should have... even as the thoughts formed they shivered and dissolved. None of them had ever stood up to their father and he doubted now that they ever would.

He opened the window and leaned out, finding some solace in the sweet air. It was almost impossible to accept that he would never see his mother again. That he would never hear her voice, never again breathe in the familiar slightly powdery smelling old-fashioned perfume that she always wore, never hold one of her neat little hands and feel the returning squeeze. He closed the window again and turned to survey the room. What would happen to the cottage now he wondered? It was slightly run-down but it was very pretty and in a very attractive location. As a weekend retreat it would be perfect. Father would probably sell it at a huge profit as a second home to one of his city friends. He sighed. If he and Em and Jacob had been in a better financial position they could have possibly bought it themselves. But they weren't in a better financial position. They were, in fact, each of them, in a very bad financial position.

At the thought of money, the despair swept through him again. Only a matter of weeks now until the auditors arrived and then the balloon would well and truly go up. He knew in his heart of hearts that he could expect no mercy from the other partners and in truth he didn't blame them. His acts of theft had put them all in jeopardy. Once word got out, people would be less willing to use the firm and they would all suffer from the loss of reputation. Well, it was at least some consolation that his mother didn't live to see her younger son go to prison. He felt his throat go dry as the word prison exploded into his brain, knocking out all other thoughts. He closed his eyes and breathed in deeply. Had Mother left any gin, he wondered? He could do with a drink. He wandered across to the kitchen and pushed open the door. There, as he suspected, stood a half-full bottle of gin on the little kitchen table. He doubted that there would be any lemons but would there be any tonic in the fridge?

Reaching across he pulled open the fridge door and swept his eye across the contents inside. Or, rather, the lack of them. A plastic bottle of milk, obviously considerably past its sell by date, stood on one shelf next to a small piece of cheese wrapped in clingfilm. On the shelf above sat a packet of sweets. He stared at it for a moment. His mother had always had a sweet tooth but if that was all she was relying on for sustenance then it was no wonder that she was so thin. Sighing, he closed the fridge door again and poured himself a large gin from the bottle on the table. In the absence of tonic he would make do with water. Right now, he thought, anything would do to dull the pain and the fear. Running a splash of water into his glass he took a huge gratifying swallow and felt some of the tension drain away. His father had always said that he was like his mother. Perhaps his father had been more right than he had realised.

CHAPTER THIRTY-TWO

JACOB LOOKED OUT across the lawns, watching the lights from the village twinkling in the distance. It had been a good idea for him and Em to walk down to the village pub. Apart from the fact that it got them out of the increasingly claustrophobic atmosphere of Seton Manor, the villagers had been nothing but kindly. Word of his mother's death had spread quickly and far from whispering behind their fingers they had all approached and spoken to them, offering their condolences and bringing their own affectionate reminiscences of his mother. While they might have tended to avoid her in later years, particularly as she drank more and more, many of them had demonstrated the sensitivity not to mention that but had talked instead of their fond memories of her in the earlier days. He had chatted with a couple of old friends from primary school too, who remembered when their mother had volunteered as a play group leader. They seemed cheerful, contented men who appeared happy with their lot. They had asked what he was doing with himself these days and he had told them that he was a senior civil servant. Which was true, in a way. He was a senior civil servant. Just not an employed one.

The Goodman's had been in the pub, too, with what he thought was their son, and they had spoken to him and Em and offered to buy them a drink. They were a nice family, he thought. Sensible and kindly. The kind of family that he would have liked to belong to. He wondered suddenly how different all their lives would have been if his father had remained a small business man, a local builder who earned a decent living but no more? If he and Emily and Edward had married locally and stayed in the village? Of course, they wouldn't have had all the advantages that had been bestowed upon them but, really, where had that got them? Emily was practically bankrupt, Edward was looking down the barrel of a long prison sentence and, unless things picked up considerably, he was destined to a life on benefits. A single life on benefits at that, as he doubted that Felicity would stay with him once the children left home. A woman who always knew where her best interest lay, he wouldn't be surprised if she'd got somebody else lined up already. She seemed to have a suspiciously large number of social engagements of late. He surprised himself by finding that he didn't really care. If Felicity found happiness with somebody else, then good luck to her.

He turned as his father came into the room. He regarded him for a moment. Somehow the old man seemed to have shrunk, he didn't appear as quite the towering figure that he had always been. He watched as he walked across the room and helped himself from the whisky decanter.

"How's Orlando?"

Not that he gave a shit but it seemed the civilised thing to say, and he hadn't quite given up hope of being bailed out financially.

"He is with his mother. Fortunately he doesn't seem to have suffered from his ordeal."

For a moment there was silence and then Sir William burst out.

"What on earth was he doing in Guido's apartment? How the hell did he get in there?"

Jacob pressed his lips together and resisted the urge to give the obvious answer, namely that Orlando was in Guido's flat because somebody had put him there. Somebody who had a key and somebody who had been hoping to extort two million quid out of Sir William. He sat down and crossed his legs at the ankle in the nonchalant way that he knew annoyed his father.

"Well, at least you won't have to pay out the two million now."

"Thank you, Jacob. That is, of course, some comfort."

Jacob suppressed a smile. His father really did take the absolute biscuit.

"But I shall find who is responsible for this," Sir William continued, his face reddening and the very slight burr of the village accent that he had worked so hard to obliterate rising to the fore in his rage. "And, by God, they will pay."

Jacob remained silent as Sir William drew in his breath and narrowed his eyes.

"And I consider it damned odd that those Goodman people seem to keep turning up everywhere. First Guido, then Elizabeth and now Orlando. I've got a good mind to go over there and speak to them, I…"

He stopped as Bridie came in leading Orlando by the hand. She propelled him gently towards his father. Sir William stooped and hugged his son to him. Jacob felt a sudden rush of jealousy. His father had very rarely hugged him like that. The only time that he could recollect him doing so was when he had given his father a home-made birthday card decorated with silver and blue stars. He would, he guessed, have been about five years old at the time. But, surely, his father must have demonstrated some physical affection at other times? If so, he couldn't recall it.

"Billy, I've ordered supper to be served in the morning room." She glanced across at Jacob, her expression cold. "For all of us," she added.

EMILY WATCHED AS Bridie leaned over and carefully cut up Orlando's food for him. For God's sake, the child was five years old and he hadn't come to any harm. In fact he appeared to have spent his so-called ordeal watching television and eating sweets. She felt her head start to ache. She could do with a couple of days watching television and eating sweets herself right now. She looked over towards Edward. He had hardly spoken since he had returned from Mummy's cottage and now he was barely touching his food. She closed her eyes briefly. She wanted to go home, to be back in her own little house with a glass of wine and a toasted cheese sandwich with the front door firmly closed, so that she could grieve for her mother alone. And yet, that image of a safe haven was, she knew, an illusion. What waited for her at home was not peace and comfort. It was more worry, more anxiety, more increasingly futile attempts to dodge her creditors. But at least, she reflected, she wasn't facing the threat of imprisonment. Not like poor Ed.

She watched as he pushed the dauphinoise potato around his plate with the edge of his fork. He looked older, the fine lines around his eyes had deepened and his mouth seemed to have lost the ability to smile. She wasn't surprised. It wasn't just their mother's death that was weighing on him, it was the threat of disgrace and with it the certainty that to all intents and purposes it would end his marriage and with it would go not just his wife but his children as well. She eyed her father as he chomped his way through his steak. Would the shame of Ed's disgrace be sufficient to make him offer to bail him out? It might be but somehow she doubted it. She sometimes had a nasty suspicion that Daddy actually rather enjoyed it when one of them came a cropper. She suspected that it made him feel superior and tightened his grip on them.

"So, has he said anything?" asked Jacob, pointing the blade of his knife towards Orlando who was now pushing food into his mouth with his fingers and dropping half of it onto the table cloth.

Bridie pursed her lips and clasped Orlando to her.

"Orlando has been severely traumatised. Billy and I have decided not to question him for the moment."

"He doesn't look very traumatised to me," said Jacob, as Orlando crammed more food into his mouth, making his cheeks bulge. Sir William laid down his knife and fork and glared at his eldest son.

"That remark is, unfortunately, typical of you, Jacob. We have no idea what this poor boy has been through but our task is to help him get over it. Which Bridie and I have decided we will not do by pestering him. However, grateful though we are that he has been found safe and well, I will not just let this matter drop. Poor Bridie has been to hell and back. To say nothing of my own distress."

"Will you inform the police now, Daddy?" asked Emily.

"That was, naturally, my first instinct, Emily. However, on reflection, I have decided not to involve them. If word of this gets out it may encourage another attempt. I think that it is better to keep it within the family. But you may be assured that whoever is the perpetrator of this crime will pay. And pay dearly."

Sir William's mouth tightened as he spoke and a chill descended across the table. For several moments they all continued eating in silence. Bored now, Orlando stopped eating and wriggled free from his mother's grasp. Struggling down from the table he began to march around the room, kicking the chair legs of the diners as he did so. Emily took a deep breath.

"Bridie, would you mind very much asking Orlando not to do that? It's rather annoying."

Bridie looked at her husband and then back again at Emily, her hard little eyes narrowed.

"He's not doing any harm. And after all that he's been through, I would have thought that for once you might have had a little…" She stopped as her eyes filled and she reached into her pocket for one of her little lace-edged handkerchiefs. Sir William reached down and scooped Orlando up just as he was about to kick his chair, and settled him on to his lap. All three of his elder children eyed the scene with cold dislike. Orlando reached across and grabbed a handful of peas from Emily's plate. Emily resisted the urge to stick her fork straight into the grasping little hand.

"Daddy," said Orlando, his high piping voice breaking into the uncomfortable silence that had fallen over the dining table. "When is Scarlett coming back?"

Sir William dipped his head and kissed his son gently on the forehead.

"I'm afraid that Scarlett had to go away, Orlando. But never mind. You'll have another nanny soon. A nice one. I expect that you'll like her much better than Scarlett

Orlando set up a loud piercing wail as big fat tears coursed down his chubby cheeks and dropped from the end of his nose. Sniffing them back he cleared his throat.

"But I love Scarlett. I told her this morning that when I'm grown up I'm going to marry her. And she said that we would have a party with balloons and chocolate cake and everything."

The words dropped like a falling stone. Bridie reached across and stroked Orlando's arm.

"I think that you've got it a bit wrong, sweetheart. You couldn't have told her this morning. You must have told her another time."

Orlando pushed his bottom lip out. Emily realised for the first time how like their father he looked. She had always thought that Orlando favoured his mother, with his small eyes and sharp nose, but today she would have known without a doubt that he was his father's son.

"I did." He twisted round to face his father. "I did tell her this morning. I said that I was going to marry her. I said it when we were in that house where the cars are. I did, Daddy."

CHAPTER THIRTY-THREE

EMILY, JACOB AND Edward sat huddled together in Jacob's room drinking the wine that they had brought up with them.

"I can hardly believe it," said Edward. "Scarlett, of all people. Although really, when you think about it, we shouldn't be surprised. She was the person who was with him the most and it follows that she probably had the best opportunity."

Emily laughed suddenly, a merry chuckle that lightened the atmosphere and wiped some of the cares from his face.

"I always did rather like her. No wonder she was so keen on Orlando. He was her golden ticket. I bet she couldn't believe her luck when she got the job here."

"It does explain a lot," said Jacob. "I mean, I know he's our half-brother and so on but he's not exactly the sort of kid that you'd take to." He paused and thought for a moment. "In actual fact, he's really the sort of kid that people very much do not take to. But apart from that, it also explains how he was persuaded away. We always said that he wouldn't have gone willingly with anyone that he didn't know. But, you know, Guido must have been in on it, too. Scarlett and Orlando were in his apartment. Guido could hardly have failed to notice them there. What do you think, Ed?"

Edward took a large gulp of his wine. In an odd way, he was enjoying the distraction of this conversation. At least it took his mind off thinking about the death of his mother and the appalling prospect of what waited for him at home. He knew, in his heart of hearts, that short of a miracle, he would have to tell Delia what he'd done as soon as he got back. He couldn't just let her find out. But right now, right at this moment, he didn't have to worry about it. He ran the little scene that had taken place downstairs back through his mind. His father had looked absolutely stunned at Orlando's announcement and for the first time that Edward had ever been aware of, he had appeared to be completely speechless. Bridie had sat equally speechless until, at last, she had stood up and swept a protesting Orlando away to his room. He and Jacob and Emily had picked up their wine glasses and sidled quietly out of the room. By unspoken consent they had made their way towards the Parsley Suite.

"I think that he must have been," said Edward, at last. He paused and thought for a moment, "I wonder how much Father and Bridie really knew about Scarlett? I mean, where she's worked before and so on."

"Father always checks everybody out," pointed out Emily. "Even people like window cleaners."

"But he might not have in this case," said Edward. "He may have left it to Bridie, thinking that it was her area or something. He can be very old-fashioned sometimes. And Bridie may have just accepted whatever references were offered her. But even if Father did check Scarlett out, there's nothing to suggest that she wasn't legit. I mean, she probably is a qualified nanny. Also, she might not have come to Seton Manor with the plan in mind. Maybe somebody suggested it to her after she arrived. Like Guido, for instance."

Jacob nodded.

"I suspect that you're right there, Ed," he said. "The two of them must have been in it together." He frowned and narrowed his eyes slightly. "But then why was Guido killed?"

"We don't know that he was," said Edward. "It may well have been natural causes."

"You don't get the kind of police turnout that we had here for natural causes," said Jacob.

Edward looked thoughtful.

"True. But whatever happened with Guido, I wonder why Scarlett suddenly decamped? She'd had the nerve to go this far, why did she suddenly give up on the plan? In a sense, the worst part was over. I mean, she must have had nerves of steel to agree to the thing in the first place. All she had to do was hold on until she got the money. And she surely to God knew that Orlando would talk. As indeed he has."

Emily nodded.

"I see what you mean. What was it that mother used to say? Something about somebody might as well be hanged for a sheep as a lamb? Once Scarlett had done the initial bit, she was already guilty of a crime." She paused. "I think. Was she, Ed?"

Emily turned to Edward, who thought for a moment. His work had been mostly in probate and trusts. His criminal law was rusty to say the least, but he was sure that even if a crime wasn't completed it would still count as something. Somewhere in the dim and dusty halls of his memory of Friday afternoon criminal law lectures, he fished out the word attempt. He was fairly sure that an attempt carried the same sentence as if the crime had actually been carried out.

"I think so, Em. I've got a vague memory of the accused having to do some act that's more than 'merely preparatory.'"

"What does that mean?" asked Jacob.

"Well, more than just thinking about it or planning it. Some positive act."

Jacob laughed.

"Well, I think that grabbing Orlando and stashing his fat little carcass in Guido's apartment would count as more than mere preparation, or whatever you call it."

"But maybe," said Emily. "Scarlett just decided that it wasn't worth it. I mean, think about it. Our father is just about the last man that you'd want to cross. Although," she added, "you'd think that she might have considered that beforehand so I suppose she must have been fairly sure that she'd get away with it."

Jacob thought for a moment about the slim curly-haired nanny with the wide smile. No wonder Orlando had loved her. He'd be in love with her himself given half the chance. And if she wasn't at least twenty years younger than him.

"Anyway," he said, "she wasn't all bad. Orlando seems to have been genuinely fond of her and he clearly hadn't come to any harm. And she left all the doors open so he could get out, Jeremy Goodman told us that. She didn't leave him locked in there, which she could easily have done. Once she'd gone, Orlando could have walked out at any time. Probably as soon as his sweets had run out."

Edward, feeling restless, got up and began walking around. He paused by the window and sat on the sill facing them, his hands palm down.

"You remember when Orlando first went missing? That morning all of us searched for him. Us three and father searched inside the house. Bridie and Guido searched outside. So why didn't Bridie find Orlando then? Surely they would have searched the garages and the apartment?"

"Elementary, my dear Watson," said Jacob, "Because he wasn't in there. He must have been taken somewhere else first and then brought back to Guido's apartment later. I mean, if he had been in Guido's apartment Bridie would have seen him.

He's not the sort of child that's hard to miss." He paused and then continued. "Scarlett hadn't been sacked at that point, or at least she hadn't left. She was still in the house, I remember seeing her when we were searching. So somebody else must have been with Orlando."

"Not necessarily," said Edward. "Whoever took him could have just dumped him somewhere with a few tons of chocolate, intending to go back later. Which could well have been Scarlett."

"But Ed," said Emily. "That would have been a huge risk for her to take. Suppose that something had happened to him?"

"It didn't though, did it? Anyway, it would only have been for an hour or so. It wasn't like he would have been left overnight or anything."

For a moment the three of them fell silent.

"It would have had to be somewhere indoors," said Emily at last. "Somewhere that he could be locked in. Otherwise he might just have simply wandered out." She paused and thought for a moment. "But if Guido was searching with Bridie, and Scarlett was still in the Manor, that must mean that, unless Orlando was left entirely alone, there was a third person involved. But who?"

"That, my dear Em," said Edward, "is the million dollar question."

CHAPTER THIRTY-FOUR

JEREMY PLACED THE last of the cases in the boot of the car and stretched his arms up high behind his head. He could feel some of the tension draining from him. It had been a stressful few days for all of them but, hopefully, it was over now. Looking around him he could see that it was going to be another golden summer day and the scenery here was undeniably beautiful, but he wanted to go home. He had slept badly last night, tossing and turning and dreaming weird dreams in which he was driving but as the car accelerated, his foot was unable to reach the brake pedal no matter how much he stretched towards it. He smiled. It didn't take a psychiatrist to work that one out. Ever since he and Carlos had discovered Guido floating in the pool everything had taken on a surreal air, almost like watching a movie in slow motion. The sooner they got away from it all, the better.

He glanced at his watch. If they got a move on they could still get going quite early, albeit not as early as they would have done if Sir William hadn't come barging in just after breakfast. He thought about their encounter. He was coming to the conclusion that Sir William, despite his veneer of affability and charm, was really a most dislikeable man. They had just finished their breakfast when he had banged on their door and then hadn't waited to be invited in but had simply barged past them into the sitting room. Molly had sent Carlos straight to his room. Sir William had clearly been in a temper and their refusal to let him interrogate Carlos had resulted in a complete dropping of the mask. He was obviously a man not accustomed to being crossed. He hadn't quite demanded that they bring Carlos out but Jeremy wouldn't have been surprised if he had. In the end it had been Molly who had persuaded him to leave, stating politely but firmly that they were on the point of departure and that Jeremy had already told him all that they knew. There was nothing to add. Sir William had left at last, leaving behind him an atmosphere of sour mistrust. Jeremy smiled to himself. Small, fair and slight of frame, Molly was completely implacable when anybody she loved was threatened.

"Jeremy, I can't find the cats. They were here just now but they seem to have disappeared."

Jeremy turned to face Carlos and groaned.

"I knew that we should have put them in their baskets last night. Where have the little sods got to, I wonder?"

"I bet they haven't gone far. Shall I go and look for them?"

"You'd better had. What's Molly doing?"

"Cleaning out the fridge."

Jeremy grinned.

"I'd better go and make sure that she doesn't leave any wine behind."

CARLOS SET OFF across the lawns, calling for Aubrey and Vincent as he ran. They wouldn't have gone far, he knew. They were probably just having a final look round before they left. To his right lay the copse. He glanced across and shivered slightly. It seemed to him that a sinister pall lay over it, a smothering blanket that smelled of death. That was where they had found Elizabeth Pelham and it was a place that he had hoped never to visit again. He slowed down to a walking pace as he advanced reluctantly towards it. He ought to check it out, he knew, but he really didn't want to. He'd do it quickly and then get out.

Stepping into the little glade where Teddy and Casper had camped, he stopped. What was that noise? A low burbling sound seemed to be coming from just behind the biggest tree, the tree behind which Elizabeth Pelham had been laying. He listened harder. It was voices he could hear, he was sure of it, but voices that sounded as though they had been lowered. He thought for a moment. Why would two people be meeting in the copse and whispering? If there was nothing wrong, why didn't they just talk normally? In his experience, people only whispered when they were up to no good. Every instinct told him to be quiet as he edged behind the tree nearest to him and dropped down to the ground. He jumped as he found himself looking into a pair of green golden eyes.

"Aubrey," he whispered, and gathered the cat to him. "Keep quiet."

Carlos strained to hear as the voices continued. He was sure that he had heard one of them before, it sounded slightly familiar, but it was so low, barely more than a whisper, that he couldn't tell if it was a man or a woman. Edging round the side of the tree he crept forward, followed by Aubrey and Vincent who had now joined them, and then dropped to his stomach. Whoever it was talking was doing something bad, he just knew it. When he had lived in Brazil, and also when he had lived in the Meadows, the only people who talked in those kind of voices were drug dealers. But surely, there weren't people dealing at Seton Manor? Although when he thought about it, it was as good a place as any. In fact, better than most. Who would suspect it of going on here? He'd even known it happen at the local swimming pool in the neighbourhood where he had first lived with Molly and Jeremy. It had been in the changing rooms and two teenaged boys, still in their swim shorts, had huddled in the corner, hair still dripping, as they exchanged small packets for money. He hadn't told Jeremy. He feared that Jeremy would think that he should do something about it and there was absolutely no point in trying to do anything. If they didn't deal at the local swimming pool, they'd simply find somewhere else. And, more to the point, Jeremy might get hurt.

 He inched forward slightly and then hesitated. Maybe, actually, on reflection, this wasn't such a good idea. What would actually be a very good idea was to make a swift exit. Whatever those people were doing was nothing to do with him and, frankly, he wanted it to remain that way. He twisted his head and glanced behind him. Could he make a retreat quietly? He thought for a moment. Perhaps a better thing would be to jump up suddenly and pretend that he was just out for a stroll. But what if they were dangerous? What if they thought he had overheard what they were saying? His experience of gang warfare both in Sao Paulo and the Meadows told him that witnesses, unwitting or otherwise, often met with a grisly end.

He had sometimes thought that it was really nothing short of a miracle how many people, when questioned by the police, had completely failed to notice when a person had been shot dead right in front of them. All right, this was the English countryside and things like that didn't happen here except on the telly where anything could happen and frequently did, but he wasn't taking any chances. As his father used to say, better a live coward than a dead hero. He thought rapidly. If he kept very quiet, he could crawl back out of the glade and run off back to the apartment. He'd found the cats, they'd follow him he knew.

He stood up and started to move backwards, lifting one foot after another in exaggerated slow motion, and then froze. One of the people was emerging from behind the tree. He held his breath and fought the temptation to close his eyes, just as he had as a child when he was hiding from Maria. Please, please, he prayed, don't let them look in this direction. The person who had emerged stood with her back to him, one hand playing with her long curly hair.

CHAPTER THIRTY-FIVE

CARLOS TWISTED HIS head and looked out of the rear window. Stretching behind them lay Seton Manor, soft and golden in the morning light but now somehow sinister, a place where bad things had happened. He hadn't told Jeremy and Molly about the strange people in the copse and he had no intention of doing so. It was probably nothing anyway and besides which, he didn't want anything to delay their departure any further. The sooner they got home, the better as far as he was concerned. Whatever the people had been up to was their business, it was nothing to do with anyone else. Anyway, there were probably all sorts of reasons why they should have been meeting in the copse and talking quietly, none of which held any interest for him.

As the Manor shrank further into the distance he felt a lightening of spirit. Soon they'd be well on their way and they could leave all this behind them. Next to him the cats lay peacefully in their baskets, the calming spray which Molly had used having worked its magic again. Carlos grinned suddenly. One of the cats was snoring. A light kerfuffle of a sound. He leaned over and listened more closely. It was Aubrey. He closed his eyes and relaxed. It was warm in the car and it made him feel sleepy. His head lolled to one side as he felt himself drift away.

He jolted suddenly awake and sat upright. A grinding noise followed by an alarming clanking sound was filling the car. A faintly acrid smell polluted the air. Pulling over, Jeremy turned off the engine and groaned.

"That's all we bloody need."

Carlos leaned forward and put his head between the front seats, looking from Molly to Jeremy.

"What is it? What's happened?"

Jeremy shrugged.

"Absolutely no idea."

"Can we fix it?"

Even as he asked the question, he knew the answer. Jeremy, while not completely impractical, usually avoided any DIY or general repairs. As he had said often enough to Molly, why do it yourself when you can pay somebody else to do it? Besides which, all he asked of any modern convenience was that you plugged it in or turned the key and it worked. How it worked was of no interest to him whatsoever. And that applied to cars, too.

"Probably not," said Jeremy. "We'll have to call the RAC." He looked out of the window at the surrounding greenery. "It would help if we knew where we are."

Carlos sat back again and pulled his phone out of his pocket. Smiling, he tapped the screen and then handed it over to Jeremy.

"Google Maps. There, the blue dot. That's where we are."

Jeremy laughed.

"Carlos, I take back everything I've ever said about your mobile."

CARLOS SAT ON the low brick wall and licked delicately at the ice cream that Molly had bought for him, twisting the cone round and round to catch the drips. At his feet sat the cats in their baskets, still asleep and apparently untroubled by all the trauma of the car breaking down and being towed to a local garage. To his right stood the town sign, the painted emblem swinging slightly in its frame. He stared at it for a moment. There was something vaguely familiar about the name of the town, but he didn't think that he'd ever been in this neck of the woods before. Perhaps he'd seen it on the news or something. He looked up as Jeremy walked towards him, his hands in his pockets, his expression glum.

"Looks like we're stuck here," said Jeremy, sitting down on the wall next to him. "Where's Molly gone?"

"To buy some sandwiches and water. What did the garage say?"

"Well, it's not terminal but the car needs some new parts, which they don't have in stock. They've ordered them but they won't be here until tomorrow."

Carlos nodded.

"What shall we do? Can we get a train home?"

"I don't think that would be very practical, Carlos. Apart from having to drag the cases around, there's the cats to consider. I think I'll have to see about hiring a car to get us back. If I've got my licence with me, that is."

He fished around in his inside jacket pocket as he spoke. Carlos watched him with interest. Jeremy was really clever and brainy and everything, but he wasn't always practical like Molly. But then, he reflected, if you had Molly you didn't need to be practical. If Jeremy didn't have his driving licence with him, it was a racing certainty that Molly would have hers.

Down at his feet, Aubrey yawned and stretched. Lifting his head he looked sleepily through the bars of his basket at the unfamiliar scene around him. This didn't look like home. It didn't matter, he could hear Carlos and Jeremy's voices so everything must be all right. Half-turning, he settled back down and fell asleep again. In the basket next to him, Vincent continued sleeping undisturbed.

"Have you got it?" Carlos asked.

Jeremy shook his head.

"No. I meant to bring it with me but I forgot."

"Why do you need it anyway? Can't you just, sort of, go and pay?"

"I don't think that you can hire a car without a current licence. I hope that Molly has got hers with her."

Carlos crunched the last of his ice cream cone while he thought about it.

"Perhaps we could find a hotel or bed and breakfast or something?"

"We could," said Jeremy. "But then again, there's the cats to consider."

"We could just sneak them in," Carlos suggested.

Jeremy laughed.

"Right. And how exactly do you suggest that we do that?"

"Well," Carlos began and then stopped as a tall man strode towards them.

"Jeremy! What on earth are you doing here?"

Jeremy got up from the wall and held out his hand.

"Hello, Jonathon. Good to see you again. I'm afraid that our car has broken down. We were on our way home. The garage have said that they can fix it but not until tomorrow. We were just discussing the possibilities of hotels for the night."

"Nonsense." Jonathon Beaumont smiled. "You must come to us. We've got plenty of room. Hold on, I'll just give Anne a ring and tell her to expect guests."

"That's very good of you," said Jeremy. "But what about the cats?"

"No problem," said Jonathon as he pulled out his mobile. "The more the merrier. And Teddy and Casper will be thrilled."

CHAPTER THIRTY-SIX

CARLOS PICKED AT his food, feeling slightly nervous. He had known that Teddy and Casper were a bit posh, but he hadn't realised that they were this posh. They actually had serving dishes on the table and matching serving dishes at that, even though it was only lunch time. Molly and Jeremy only used serving dishes when they had people round to dinner. Other than that it was usually put straight on to plates with the three of them eating at the kitchen table while they talked about what they'd been up to that day. And when he had lived with Maria they had generally eaten off trays on their laps, especially in the winter when they had tried to heat only one room at a time. The flat had central heating but in those very early days they never turned it on, making do instead with a two bar electric fire and even that only on the coldest of days. He shouldn't have been surprised about Teddy and Casper though. He had first met them when they were boarding at Arcadia Academy, a fee-paying school with the emphasis on the fees.

He turned his head slightly to one side and looked out through the open French windows to the huge garden beyond. The big velvety roses tumbled over the trellises and the green stripes on the lawn looked as though they had been painted on. It appeared like something out of a magazine. They probably had a gardener. And a cleaner. He smiled slightly to himself. This was exactly the kind of house in which his mother had loved working as a cleaner herself, coming home and filling his head with stories of beautiful furniture and expensive paintings, thrilled when one of her employers had given her some cast-off clothing or leftovers from a dinner party carefully wrapped in foil for her to take home. What would she think if she could see him now, actually sitting at the table with the kind of people who had once employed her? He smiled to himself. She would probably have told him to make sure he kept his mouth shut when he was eating.

He glanced across the table to where Teddy and Casper were sitting. On arrival, they had rushed out to meet him as Jonathon's car crunched across the gravel drive, feet flying as they ran towards him, and pulling open the car doors almost before it had stopped. The anxiety of the last few days had evaporated completely and he had stumbled out towards them in a great rush of happiness. He should have known as soon as he saw the town sign that it was near where Teddy and Casper lived but, on reflection, maybe it wasn't that surprising that he hadn't recognised it. He and Teddy never wrote letters, although they had talked of doing so once. But somehow they never had and although he knew her address, he didn't think that he had ever used it. They emailed or WhatsApped or texted.

"It's so nice to meet you at last, Carlos," said Teddy's mother, passing him a dish of potato salad. He eyed it with interest. If he had to put money on it, he'd say that it was home-made. Those were definitely fresh chives on the top. Did they, he wondered, come from their garden? Perhaps when he had his restaurant, he'd have a kitchen garden too. He'd never actually grown anything before. In fact, until he had gone to live with Molly and Jeremy, he'd never had a garden before. In Brazil they'd lived in an apartment high in the sky and when he and Maria had lived in the Meadows the green space around the flats had been mostly colonised by rusting cars and discarded syringes. But, really, how hard could growing things be? He was sure that if he put his mind to it he could do it. There was bound to be books and stuff about it. Molly was the gardener in the family. He'd ask her when he got home.

"I've heard so much about you," Anne continued, breaking into his thoughts. Carlos looked at her warily. "And you've been such a good influence on Casper."

Carlos blinked in surprise. Had he? Well, if that's what she thought, he wasn't about to contradict her although he suspected somebody of having given him a very good press. Casper smiled at him, the wide-eyed bright innocent smile that made him look like the poster boy for healthy breakfast cereals and which he used to such excellent effect.

"Yes," said Jonathon in agreement. "He really does seem to have turned a corner lately." He glanced at his son and crinkled his brow in a mock frown. "Let's hope it lasts this time."

Carlos looked at Teddy and Casper's father. He looked like such a nice man. Sort of quite big and grave but kindly. The kind of man that would bung you fifty pence on penny for the guy night or teach you how to ride a bike without shouting at you. The kind of man that you could turn to if you were in trouble. The kind of man, in fact, that was in stark contrast to his own father, or bum-face as his mother had frequently referred to him although privately he had often thought that was disrespectful to bums.

How many times, he wondered, had he lain in the dark in his bed in Brazil listening to his father's drunken rantings and his mother crying? How many times had his father punched him in the head for daring to exist? Or cracked him across the back of his legs with his big leather belt? But never when his mother was present. Even his father wouldn't have dared to touch him if Maria had been there. He'd only done it once and Maria had leapt up and whopped him straight across the back of the head with a big heavy saucepan. He sighed inwardly. It was all such a matter of chance who you got born to. Like, he could just as well have been born into royalty or something. He could have lived in a palace and had a crown and that. But, he reflected, suddenly cheering up, he had the Goodmans now. Jeremy and Molly, as well as Aubrey and Vincent, and they were miles better than any old royalty.

"It was so sad to hear about dear Elizabeth Pelham," said Anne, looking across to Molly and Jeremy. "I gather that she had a heart attack."

Casper laid down his knife and fork, his expression one of abject disappointment.

"I thought that she was done in."

Anne sighed.

"No, Casper, she was not done in, as you so elegantly express it. I heard from Connie Chambers, who heard it from the vicar, that she died of natural causes. I'm not surprised, though. She's had a weak heart for years and she did drink rather too much, although I can't say that I blame her. She'd been through the mill a bit in recent years." She paused for a moment and then continued. "We were actually quite good friends at one time. She was older than me but we got on awfully well. It was such a shame, when the Pelham's divorced she seemed to drift off into a world of her own. I went over to see her once, you know, in that little cottage she lived in. I'm sure that she was at home but she didn't answer the door. I felt rather a fool just standing there knocking so I went away again. But in her day, she was good fun and she did an awful lot of work for local charities. In fact, that was where I met her. We were invited to one of her charity balls over at Seton Manor. Why on earth Sir William left her and married that Bridie woman I shall never know."

"I think that we may hazard a guess," said Jonathon and grinned.

"Jonathon," Anne's voice held a warning note as she glanced over to Teddy and Casper. "Didn't the Pelham's nanny work for that friend of yours, Teddy? The one that lives over in Maybrick village?" she continued.

"Yes." Teddy nodded. "Scarlett. She's really nice. She was the nanny to Clarice, Amy's little sister. I think that it was her first job. She used to let us play with her make-up when Amy's parents were out."

"Well, I think she's got her work cut out with that youngest boy of Sir William's. From all I've heard, he's an absolute horror," said Jonathon.

Molly, Jeremy and Carlos exchanged glances. Clearly, Teddy and Casper hadn't told their parents what they'd overheard at the hotel and the news of the kidnapping of Orlando and his subsequent release hadn't travelled this far by any other route. Best way really, thought Jeremy. It was none of anybody's business, the boy had been found safe and sound and, as his mother used to say, least said soonest mended.

Anne laid her knife and fork down and leaned back in her chair.

"If everybody's finished, why don't we take some drinks outside while the sun's still shining? Casper, you can show Carlos the little summer house that you're converting." She turned to Carlos and smiled. "It's rather tumble down and we'd more or less stopped using it since the new one was built but Casper is going to turn it into an outdoor study in preparation for his exams next year. He thinks that it would help to have somewhere quiet and away from distractions. It's his new project. We're so pleased that he's taking an interest in academic matters at last."

Teddy looked at her mother fondly. Grown-ups were such innocents. Casper's little summer house was actually his headquarters for the international detective agency that he was in the process of setting up. His first case was to be the discoverer of Orlando's kidnapper and he had already, unknown to his parents, been getting quotes online from electricians to get power out there for the bank of computers he intended to install.

CHAPTER THIRTY-SEVEN

CARLOS FELT HIMSELF relax as he followed his friends out into the garden. They might be a bit posh, but they were still Teddy and Casper. Teddy caught him by the hand.

"There's a stream that runs through the bottom of the garden. I'll show you." Without waiting for an answer, she pulled him along behind her. "Come on, Casper."

The stream glittered in the sunlight as the three of them flopped down beside it, the clean clear water rippling over the stones as it tripped along its route down to the river. Casper rolled onto his back and stared up at the sky for a moment before turning on his side and propping himself up on one elbow to face Carlos.

"We found out some stuff about that handy bloke. How he died and some other stuff."

"He means Guido," said Teddy. "And we didn't exactly find it out Casper, Daddy was talking to Mummy and we were listening. Not outside doors or anything," she hastened to assure Carlos. "They were talking about it over dinner last night. I was going to message you today about it."

"What did they say?"

"Well, Daddy said that he'd been for a drink with some friend of his. A friend of Daddy's that is, not the handyman."

Carlos nodded. It was weird how grown-ups always seemed to have friends who knew things. Although, when he thought about it, teenagers did too although sometimes some of the things they knew were not the sort of things that you actually wanted to know anything about. He looked at Teddy as she tipped her face up towards the sun. The tiny fork-shaped scar under her chin showed more clearly today. He had asked her once how she had got it and she had told him that she had been jumping over a low wall and the grass was wet. Her foot had slipped and she had banged her chin down on the brick. Her mother had rushed her to hospital where they had cleaned and stitched the wound and stuck some plaster stuff over it. When the plaster had been removed she had been left with little white whisps, just like a beard she said. Carlos wouldn't care if she had ten beards. He loved her, he knew, with all his heart. And he always would.

"Anyway," continued Teddy, unaware of the silent assertion of love that had just been declared, "this friend of Daddy's is something to do with the city hospital. He's a consultant or something. He said that Guido's medical notes said that he'd been in the army. And that he'd been all over the world and fought in wars and things. He knew because Guido suffered an injury in one of them."

"I didn't think that we had wars anymore," said Casper. "I thought that was just in the old days."

"There's always wars, Casper," said Teddy. "Anyway, this friend of Daddy's said that Guido hadn't died of natural causes or an accident or anything."

"That means that he was killed," said Casper.

Teddy raised her eyebrows.

"Yes, well, I think that Carlos could have worked that one out himself, Casp."

"How was he killed? Does your dad know?" asked Carlos.

Teddy nodded.

"He said that he was shot in the back of the head, but at really close range, and that he must have then fallen or been pushed into the swimming pool."

Carlos thought for a moment.

"What sort of gun, did he say?"

Although, he reflected, if Guido had been shot at really close range it wouldn't much matter what sort of gun it was.

Teddy shook her head.

"No, Daddy didn't say."

"So, did he die from the gun shot or did he drown?"

"Daddy's friend said that it was likely that the impact of the gun shot had toppled him into the water and that he drowned. But," she added, "if he hadn't drowned then he would probably have died from being shot."

"It's odd though, isn't it," said Casper, sitting up. He crossed his legs and pulled his notebook out of his pocket. "I mean, Carlos, you said that you heard something before daybreak. So, what was the handy bloke doing out by the pool at that time?"

Teddy looked at Casper with something approaching respect.

"You know Casper, sometimes you're not as stupid as you look. Fortunately," she added. "But you're right. What on earth was he doing out at the pool that early in the morning?"

"Maybe he was going to have a swim?" suggested Casper. "You know, before all the hotel guests got in the pool or something."

Carlos shook his head.

"No, I don't think so. When I saw him in the water he was wearing jeans and a sort of checked shirt. And he had trainers on." He thought for a moment. "And there wasn't a towel on the side or anything like that. At least, I don't think there was."

"Right." Casper looked thoughtful. "Did you notice anything else?"

"Like what?" asked Carlos.

"I don't know," said Casper. "Anything." He flicked his notebook over to a new page. "Start at the beginning."

Carlos ran his mind back to that night, flicking through the pictures until he found what he was looking for. He had discovered early on in life that he had a very visual memory and he could easily call up images whenever he wanted. Being able to memorise pages of text was a talent that stood him in very good stead when it came to sitting examinations.

"Well, I was woken up by what sounded like a gun shot. Or a car back-firing. Something like that." He realised suddenly that Teddy and Casper probably didn't know what a gun shot sounded like, not a real one. "You know, like a sort of echoey bang. Then I couldn't get back to sleep so I got up to get a glass of water." He waited for a moment for Casper to catch up. "And I took it into the sitting room and looked out over the balcony and that's when I saw him. He was floating in the water, face down. I didn't realise at first what I was looking at so I just sort of stood there and stared. And the water around him was coloured. Darker than the rest of the water, although it got paler as it sort of spread out."

Casper looked up from his notebook, pen poised.

"Go on. What did you do then?"

"I went and woke Jeremy up and then we went down to the pool together and looked."

"Right." Casper nodded and tipped his head to one side. "So when you went down to the pool, did you notice anything else? Apart from Guido, I mean."

Carlos thought harder. The scene was vivid in his mind now. The dawn had been breaking and there had been the sound of bird song coming from the trees. The light was that sort of pearly light when it's not night anymore but it's not day either. He and

Jeremy had stood there silently for a moment, staring at the body, unable to look away. Then Jeremy had told him to go back inside and that he would call the police. He suddenly remembered that as he had turned to follow Jeremy he had stumbled slightly over what looked like a fishing net. But not a child's net. Not the kind of thing that you'd mess about in rock pools with. It was bigger than that, and next to it stood a big plastic tub of something.

"There was a fishing net," he said slowly. "I almost tripped over it. And a tub of something. I don't know what."

"A fishing net?" Teddy's brow crinkled. "Why would there be a fishing net out there? There's nothing to fish in a swimming pool."

Casper jumped suddenly to his feet.

"Yes there is. I know what Guido was doing out there."

"What?"

"He was cleaning the pool. And," he added triumphantly, "he was doing it at that time because it was before all the hotel guests woke up."

CHAPTER THIRTY-EIGHT

CARLOS TIPTOED QUIETLY downstairs and gently turned the handle of the utility room door. He had promised Molly that he would take responsibility for the cats and had set the alarm on his phone so that he could get up extra early to feed them. He crept further into the room and picked up the packet of cat biscuits sitting on the shelf, looking around him as he did so. He didn't want to alarm them by startling them, but he couldn't see them. They seemed to have just vanished into thin air. He stood still for a moment, puzzled. There was no way out of the utility room other than by the window and that was closed, so they couldn't be far away. Wherever they were, he hoped with all his heart that they weren't up to any mischief.

Teddy's mother had been fine about them staying but Molly had insisted that they be confined to one room, just in case they got alarmed at yet more new surroundings and tried to run away she said. Carlos had thought that it was more likely, having seen some of the expensive and beautiful furnishings in Anne and Jonathon's home, that she wasn't prepared to take the risk of the cats damaging anything. Not that they would do it on purpose, but they were sometimes a bit careless. Like that time Aubrey had jumped up at a fly near the window and brought the curtain pole crashing down, taking a vase full of daffodils with it.

Shaking the packet of cat biscuits gently, he advanced further into the room and then suddenly spun round. There they were, sitting high up on one of the shelves watching him, bunched in between packets of laundry tablets and cans of furniture polish, their eyes gleaming and their tails hanging down.

"Morning Aubrey. Morning Vincent."

He shook a pile of biscuits into their two feeding bowls and stood back as Aubrey and Vincent jumped gracefully from the shelf and made towards him. He leaned over and ran his hand over Vincent's back.

"I hope you're happy here, because we're staying a bit longer. The bad news is that you can't go out. But at least you've got your bowls and food and that."

He stood back and watched them as they settled down to their breakfast. They'd be all right. They had their litter trays and they could always climb back into their baskets for safety if they got spooked by anything. And it was only for a few days. He smiled suddenly and wrapped his arms around himself in an instinctive hug. Three more days with Teddy. Three whole days. He had hardly believed his luck when Teddy's mother had suggested over breakfast that they stay a bit longer, that they complete the remainder of their holiday with them.

"Honestly, Molly, it would be no trouble. It's such a shame that you've had your holiday cut short and as luck would have it, I'm free myself this week. We could take you out and about a bit, show you the sights. How are you fixed for the next few days, Jonathon?"

She turned to her husband who smiled in agreement.

"I've got plenty of leave owing. In fact I was thinking only the other day that if I don't start taking some of it I'll lose it. And it's pretty quiet in the office at the moment."

"Are you not sitting this week?" Anne asked. "Or have you finished for the summer?"

Carlos looked at Jonathon. Of course he was sitting. He was sitting right now, like the rest of them. What was Mrs Beaumont talking about? Noticing his confusion, Anne smiled.

"Jonathon is a magistrate, Carlos. He sits on the bench."

Carlos nodded and smiled, although inside he felt none the wiser. Was this something to do with football? Wasn't Mr Beaumont a bit old for that? Although, now he thought about it, he did know what a magistrate was. He just didn't know that they sat on benches. He thought that they sat on chairs like everybody else. Magistrates were sort of like judges. They ran the Youth Court. In fact, now he thought about it, one of them had come to Sir Frank's to give a talk to Year Ten. A tall gangly man, he appeared to be on first name terms with most of his audience, some of whom had given him a cheery welcome.

"No," said Jonathon in reply to Anne. "I'm free this week. Tell you what," he said, leaning over and pouring Jeremy more coffee, "there's a cricket match taking place in Maybrick village. It's a veterans match and one of my friends is playing. We could take a spin over and watch the game, Maybrick's not far away. The club usually run a very good bar. We could make a day of it. What do you think?"

"I suspect," said his wife, noticing the slightly disappointed look on Molly's face, "that Molly might prefer to do something else. Tell you what, why don't you take Jeremy and the children to the cricket match and I'll take Molly into town." She turned to Molly. "There are still quite a few independent shops there and there's a garden centre as well with a lovely coffee shop."

"That sounds great," said Jeremy. "What do you think, Carlos? Would you like to do that or would you rather I picked up the car and we made for home?"

Jeremy's lips twitched slightly as he spoke. Carlos looked at him suspiciously. Was he making fun? Turn down the chance for another three days with Teddy? Fat chance.

CARLOS PEERED OUT from under the brim of the straw hat that Teddy's father had lent him to shield his eyes from the sun. He didn't really get this cricket thing but there was, he had to admit, something very peaceful about it. It wasn't like football and rugby matches and that. It was... he searched for the right word. Civilised. That was it. It was civilised. He watched as a small, rather portly, man with grey hair and dressed in white took a run up and threw a ball for another man dressed in white to hit with his bat. The other team members seemed to just sort of stand around. There was something very relaxing about it though. Nobody seemed to be shouting or fighting. Nobody had even sworn at anybody yet. He could see why Jeremy and Jonathon liked it. Maybe he could ask Jeremy to teach him how to play. Or maybe there was a club that he could join at college. There was a club for everything else. Up until now he had generally avoided any form of organised games, his experience at Sir Frank's having taught him that most team games were in fact a form of blood sport, but this seemed different. To his left, Jeremy sat in his deckchair with his legs stretched out and sipped at the foaming beer that Jonathon had brought over for him. He looked, Carlos thought, more relaxed than he had ever seen him.

To his right, Teddy and Casper sat on the grass and watched the match. Slung down next to Casper was his small nylon rucksack that he carried everywhere with him. It contained, he had told Carlos, all the kit that he might need when he was detecting and he had shown him the contents. Carlos had been impressed, particularly with the roll of Sellotape that Casper said was for collecting DNA. The packet of Rolos Carlos wasn't quite so sure of but Casper had assured him that if he were stranded up a mountainside in the middle of winter, he would need the carbohydrates to stay alive.

"Because you see, Carlos, it just might happen," Casper had explained. "You just might end up stuck up some mountain in the snow and be thinking, where is Casper with his Rolos when I need him?"

And Carlos, ever fair, had to agree that although it was long shot, it just might happen one day.

Teddy sat with her arms stretched behind her, propped up on her hands. She had made a daisy chain and plaited it through her hair. Sitting there with her long sky blue cotton summer dress spread out around her with flowers in her hair, she looked, Carlos thought, like he imagined that fairy queen that Jeremy had told his class about. The one that go tricked into falling in love with a horse or a donkey or something. He reached into his pocket for his phone and quietly took a photograph of her. He would email it to himself and print it and put it on his bedroom wall when he got home. Maybe he would buy a frame or something for it. He studied the picture more closely, bringing his phone right up to his eyes so that he could examine it in detail. It was, he had to admit, a good photograph. It was so very Teddy. He started to shove the phone back in his pocket and then stopped. Was it allowed to just take pictures of somebody without them knowing? Like was it against the law or something? He thought about it for a moment. There were some photographs that definitely weren't allowed, he knew.

Some of the boys at Sir Frank's had been guilty of it and had taken some really nasty photographs of girls at school, secretly holding their phones under their desks so they could take pictures of their knickers. One of the girls had started crying when she discovered what they had been doing but they just laughed at her. It was small satisfaction that the ringleader had later been expelled for bullying some of the younger boys. By that time he had distributed the photographs he had taken all round his year group. It was not long after that, Carlos suddenly realised, that most of the girls had taken to wearing trousers to school. And at college last term all the boys on his course had been given a talk about something called appropriate behaviour by one of the personal tutors. The girls had been given a talk as well but he didn't know if it was the same one that the boys had. He'd been too shy to ask any of them.

He looked at the photograph again. He would dearly like to keep it but maybe he shouldn't. He'd show her the picture, he decided, and if she didn't like it he would delete it.

He looked up as Jonathon and Jeremy stood up.

"Good match," said Jeremy, finishing his beer. "Did you enjoy it?"

"Yeah, good," said Carlos. "It was good." He wasn't quite sure who had won, but it was true that he had enjoyed watching.

"What would you like to do now?" asked Jonathon. "Take a stroll round the village? It's very picturesque and I need to walk some of this beer off before I get back behind the wheel."

"Great idea," said Jeremy. "Are you up for that, Carlos?"

Carlos nodded. He was getting into this countryside stuff. There was a lot more going on than he'd thought.

"There's a lovely church," said Teddy. "It's really old. Sixteenth century or something."

"And it's got a graveyard," added Casper. "With graves in it."

Teddy gave him a withering look, of the kind that teenage girls reserve for younger brothers.

"No shit, Sherlock, Sorry Daddy," she added.

CHAPTER THIRTY-NINE

THE CHURCH WAS cool and dim after the bright heat of the day outside. The afternoon sunlight filtered gently through the stained glass windows, casting multi-coloured jewels of dappled light across the old oak pews. A faint aroma of beeswax hung in the air and mingled with the scent of the flowers arranged on the alter. Jeremy breathed in the familiar smell, reminiscent of the family church of his childhood where he'd sat on Sunday mornings with his brother, sandwiched between his parents and only half-listening to the sermon while he planned his first trip to space.

He looked up at the big memorial stones set high with their curly lettering and elaborately carved masonry. Only the people with money had those. The humbler folk were lucky if they got a plain inscription on a headstone. The very humble folk got nothing at all but were simply placed in unmarked graves. And he guessed that then, as now, fortunes could be as easily lost as made. He found himself suddenly thinking about Elizabeth Pelham. She had gone from being, literally, the lady of the manor to the humble tenant living in a tiny cottage on the edge of the estate. And she only had that by permission of her former husband. What sort of funeral or memorial would she have, he wondered? Not the grand affair that it might have been had she still been married to Sir William, that was for sure.

He wandered over to a pew and sat down. Poor Lady Pelham. She had been such a total wreck, in every sense of the word, the night of Sir William's birthday. It had been hard not to feel sorry for her, even though she had been behaving rather badly. And the next time that he had seen her she was dead. He hoped that it had been quick, that she hadn't had time to be frightened. She hadn't looked frightened, he recalled. In fact she had looked peaceful as she lay there in the summer sunshine. He closed his eyes briefly. He was reaching the age where death was, not exactly something to be contemplated in the near future, but definitely a reality. Unlike when he was young. When he was young, he had been going to live forever. Just like all young people.

He opened his eyes again and looked away to his left where a large polished wooden board was mounted on the wall, its gold lettering commemorating those that had died in the first war. The names were placed in alphabetical order, followed by their age and rank. There were another group of young people who had never considered their own mortality, although their deaths had not been the result of accident or disease but, rather, the politics of battling societies. His heart sank as he noted how often the same name appeared. Brothers, or fathers and sons he supposed. One poor family appeared to have lost three men. Those families must have lived in dread of the telegram boy appearing, watching fearfully as he propped up his bicycle, straightened his hat, and rapped at their door.

It was, he reflected not for the first time, all such a dreadful waste. What would those young men have thought, he wondered, if somebody had told them that it was going to happen all over again not much more than twenty years later? Would they have been so keen to enlist? When he was a teenager and working on a project about the first world war at school, his father had told him about the Pals battalions. Recruitment officers had encouraged local lads from various towns and villages, or sometimes the same place of work, to enlist together so that they could serve alongside their friends and neighbours in this great big adventure called war. Apart from the cynicism involved, what nobody had seemed to foresee was the fact that some communities lost most of their young men. And with their loss went some of the hopes and the dreams of the young women too.

He looked over to where Carlos was standing with Teddy, reading the visitors book, their heads bent together in concentration. The men that had died had been not much older than those two. Some had been even younger, having lied about their age in order to enlist. He felt a sudden lump in his throat.

"What do you think, Jeremy?" asked Jonathon, walking over to him and waving his arms around. "It must be one of the few remaining churches that isn't kept locked. It's rather lovely, isn't it?"

"It certainly is," said Jeremy, glad of the distraction. It wasn't a day to be having gloomy thoughts.

Jonathon smiled and then looked thoughtfully across to Teddy and Carlos.

"You know, they didn't say much when I picked them up from Seton Manor. I would have thought that Casper especially would have been full of it, given his rather worrying interest in all things crime-related. But they barely said a word. In fact, they've been remarkably quiet ever since they've been home. If I didn't know better, I'd think that they had a secret." He paused for a moment. "Did something happen at Seton Manor? Apart from the handy man being found dead in the pool, that is."

Jeremy swallowed. Given that he had been asked the direct question, he really felt that he couldn't lie to Jonathon. He would have to tell him about Orlando. Anyway, what harm could it do now? The boy had been found safe and well and hopefully the whole sorry business was all over. After all, he hadn't promised Sir William and it wasn't like he owed the man anything. In fact, Sir William had been border line obnoxious that last time they had met. He cleared his throat.

"Well, yes, as a matter of fact something did."

Jonathon stood quietly and waited for Jeremy to continue.

"It was to do with Orlando," said Jeremy.

Jonathon looked puzzled.

"Orlando? That brat of Sir William's?"

Jeremy nodded.

"Yes. That brat of Sir William's. He was kidnapped and the kidnappers were demanding a ransom."

Jonathon sank slowly down next to Jeremy and stared at him, momentarily silenced.

"So what happened?" he asked eventually. "How much did they ask for? Did he pay the money?"

Jeremy shook his head.

"They asked for two million but he didn't pay it. He didn't need to in the end. The boy was discovered. By Carlos as a matter of fact."

"Where was he?"

"In the handy man's apartment."

Jonathon crinkled his brow.

"What was Carlos doing in the handy man's apartment?"

Jeremy thought for a moment. This was getting complicated. Probably better not to mention Aubrey and Vincent's role in it. Jonathon would think that they were all bonkers.

"I'm not sure. I think that he just saw a door open and looked inside."

"Right." Jonathon nodded. "Well, if I'm honest, I don't hold much brief for William Pelham. Our paths have crossed a few times and I can't say that I ever took to the man. Having said that, I wouldn't have wished this on him. I wonder why the children didn't tell us about it? Talking of which," Jonathon looked around him. "Where are they?"

"I don't know where Casper is but Teddy and Carlos were here a moment ago," said Jeremy. "They've probably gone out to look at the church yard."

CHAPTER FORTY

OUTSIDE, CARLOS AND Teddy picked their way through the overgrown graves. Carlos looked about him with interest. He didn't think that he'd ever been in an English church yard before. When his mother had died, Jeremy and Molly had arranged for her to be buried in the local authority cemetery, so that he would, as they said, have somewhere to visit if he wanted to. And he had visited, quite often, particularly in the early days, catching the bus there and often walking back so that he could think about things without the distraction of other people around him. He had liked the local authority cemetery, it was peaceful, albeit rather regimented, and it was certainly well-tended. In a strange way he had quite enjoyed his trips over there. It had made him feel close to his mother again. The only other cemetery that he had known was the one in Sao Paulo, the cemetery where his grandfather was buried.

The cemetery in Sao Paulo was big and bustling, with people milling about and chatting. While some of the citizens might not have had much money, they didn't hold back when it came to funerals. The statuary was big and ornate and many of the plots were adorned with fresh flowers which indicated regular visitors. A number of the graves had small portraits of the deceased, too, set into the headstones or standing in little frames. He had enjoyed looking at them while his mother busied herself tending to his grandfather's grave, clearing away the weeds and replacing the dead flowers. He had liked to compare the names on the headstones to the faces in the portraits and wondering what sort of lives they had led. When they visited it had often been quite busy and his mother had frequently stopped to talk to people that she knew. The place he was in now was quiet and still except for the faint burbling of insects, and the air seemed hardly to move. There was nobody about apart from themselves.

From the look of them, most of the graves appeared to be very old, the stone crumbling in places and the letters faded so that on some stones they were practically illegible. Apart from a small group in the far corner, there were no new headstones. Perhaps more people got cremated in England. Or maybe this graveyard was full up. He'd ask Jeremy later, he would be bound to know. He leaned over and read the inscription on the headstone in front of him. "Here lies Jonas Barrow. Faithful to the end'. Faithful to what, Carlos wondered. He peered more closely at the inscription. It was dated 1752. He straightened up again. Actually, this place was quite sad. A number of the headstones looked as though they were about to topple over and most of them were overgrown with weeds. But, to be fair, he thought, most of the people in there had died hundreds of years ago, so there was probably nobody left to tend to them now.

Jeremy had once told him that in the old days people pretty much stayed in the village or town where they were born. They lived their lives there, got married, had children and then died. Even going to the nearest city was a big adventure. They didn't stay now though, he knew. They grew up and left, they went off to universities or new jobs and started new lives. They rarely came back. A bit like himself, he supposed. When he and Maria had arrived in England, it had never been their intention to go back to Brazil. And now, after everything that had happened, he thought it was unlikely that he would ever visit his birth place again. Or would want to, really. He had no relatives that he was aware of. There would be nothing to go back to. Anyway, England was his home now. It was where he belonged. With Molly and Jeremy.

At his side, Teddy knelt and began reading out loud from a headstone.

"Oh, Carlos, listen. This poor girl. Clara something. I can't quite read the inscription. But she was only seventeen when she died."

She turned a mournful face towards him, the daisies that she had picked earlier still entwined in her hair albeit slightly wilted now.

"What do you think she died from?"

"Some disease from the old days, I suppose." He tried to think of a disease that people used to die from. "Small pox or the black death or something."

"Do you want to see the place where they keep the coffins?"

He turned as Casper appeared grinning at his shoulder.

"What do you mean?"

"Over there, see?"

Carlos looked over in the direction that Casper was pointing. A small timber-framed building infilled with red brick stood in the corner of the church yard.

"It's called a bier house. Most churches don't have them anymore."

Carlos frowned.

"A beer house? In a church yard?"

Teddy jumped up and brushed the earth from her dress with the palms of her hands.

"No, bier, not beer. It's spelled differently."

For a moment Carlos felt quite disappointed. A beer house in a grave yard could be a good thing. It would mean that more people visited anyway.

"It's the stand thing that they put coffins on," Teddy continued. "Nowadays most dead people are kept at the undertakers. But in the old days people used to keep the bodies at home and put them in the front parlour so that people could visit them."

Carlos felt a slight shudder of revulsion. Visiting dead bodies in their coffins wasn't his idea of a good day out.

"Then," Teddy continued, "on the night before the funeral they used to take them to the bier house ready for the next day. Something like that, anyway."

"It's all right, Carlos," said Casper. "There aren't any coffins in them these days. Come on."

The three of them strolled across to the little building, the sun still beating down on the tops of their heads even though the afternoon was beginning to fade now. Carlos suddenly stopped. He could hear a raised voice and it was coming from the bier house. He motioned to Teddy and Casper to stay silent and then crept forward. Following his lead, they crept behind him. The door to the bier house stood open and as they approached one of the voices grew louder. Teddy clutched at Carlos's arm.

"It's Sir William," she whispered. "I know it is. What's he doing in the bier house?"

Moving as silently as only teenagers intent on not being discovered can, they tiptoed forward. Carlos stopped again. This really wasn't such a good idea. He had hoped that he had seen the last of Sir William and he didn't want to be discovered apparently spying on him. Besides which, only yesterday Teddy's mother had said what a good influence he was having on Casper. She wouldn't think that he was such a good influence if he brought Sir William's wrath down on his head. He turned to look at Casper. He was such an innocent really. For all his showing off and big talk, he knew nothing of the real ways of the world. And, he thought, long may it remain so. And he had to look after Teddy, too. She was older than Casper but no more worldly wise. He retreated out of earshot of the occupiers of the bier house and beckoned Teddy and Carlos to follow him.

He lowered his voice to a conspiratorial murmur.

"I think that we should just leave whoever it is to it. It's not really any of our business. Come on, let's go back to the church. Jeremy and your dad will be wondering where we are."

He half-turned and then stopped as Teddy touched his arm.

"If it's Sir William it might be to do with Orlando's kidnapping," said Teddy.

"But Orlando has been found now," said Carlos. "All that's done, it's finished."

"Yes," said Teddy. "But that doesn't mean that Sir William will just let it go. I once heard Daddy say that he's famous for bearing grudges. According to Daddy, Sir William once waited seventeen years to get his own back on someone who cheated him on a business deal. He made him bankrupt or something. Anyway, don't you want to know?"

"We might find out some interesting stuff," said Casper. "I reckon that we should stay and listen for a while."

"Yes, well, Casp," said Teddy. "That is rather your speciality."

Carlos hesitated. What excuse would they make if Sir William suddenly came out and found them hanging around? Suddenly he felt a flash of anger. What business was it of Sir William's what they were doing? If they wanted to explore a country church yard that was up to them. They had as much right to be there as he did. He didn't own the place. That was the trouble with men like Sir William he thought. They always thought that they were in charge. And, annoyingly, usually they were.

"Actually," said Teddy. "I think that Carlos is right. It's nothing to do with us. We ought to go back. Daddy and Mr Goodman will be getting worried about us."

Carlos looked at her gratefully. Sensing his unease, she had immediately stepped in to support him.

"Come on, Casp," Teddy continued.

"You go on ahead. I'll catch up in a minute," said Casper. "I just want to check something on my phone."

CHAPTER FORTY-ONE

IN THE DUSTY and rather cobwebby headquarters of the Casper Beaumont International Detective Agency, Carlos, Teddy and Casper sat on deckchairs around the small folding picnic table that was currently in use as the chief executive's desk.

"What is it, Casp?" asked Teddy. "It had better be quick, Mummy will be calling us in for dinner soon. And don't forget that Daddy is already cross with you for going off on your own."

"I didn't go off on my own," Casper protested. "I was in the church yard. If anybody went off on their own it was you."

Carlos half-smiled to himself as he listened to them squabbling. There was actually something quite soothing about it. Would they, he wondered, still be doing it when they got old? Like about thirty or something? Somehow he couldn't imagine either of them growing old. Although, if it came to it, he couldn't imagine himself growing old either. Growing old was what other people did. He let the sound of their voices wash over him as he thought about the afternoon. It had been, on the whole, quite perfect. Until they had heard the voice of Sir William that is.

"Yes well, you knew very well that Daddy wanted to get back in time to avoid the rush hour, "Teddy continued. "You know how he hates sitting in traffic. And also it's bad for the environment."

Casper stuck his tongue out.

"He could have rung me," he said.

"He did ring you," said Teddy. "We all did. It kept going to voice mail. You must have had your phone on silent. Anyway, where were you?"

"Round the back of the bier house, where all the long grass is. And you'll never guess what?"

Casper beamed at them, his eyes bright.

Teddy looked at him suspiciously.

"What?"

Without speaking, Casper picked up his phone which had been lying face down on the picnic table. Flipping it over he touched the screen and held it up for them to see. Small pictures flickered into view.

"Casper," Teddy sounded shocked. "You know that you're not supposed to record people without their permission. Mummy and Daddy have told you about it before. It's against the law." She turned to Carlos. "Isn't it?"

Carlos shrugged his shoulders and spread his hands out.

"To be honest, I'm not sure. Probably."

Casper stood up and swept the phone into his pocket.

"Well, if you don't want to know…"

Teddy looked at him, her face expressionless. For several seconds the three of them sat in silence.

"Is it Sir William?" asked Teddy at last.

Casper nodded.

"When you and Carlos went off on your own," he began. Carlos suppressed a smile. Casper absolutely never missed a trick. He'd make a great lawyer one day. Either that or he'd be serving time as a criminal mastermind, if the authorities ever managed to catch him. "I walked round the side of the bier house, you know, where it's all overgrown with weeds and stuff. And there's a window with a pane of glass missing so I just held the phone up and pressed record."

"Casp, what would you have done if Sir William had seen you?" Teddy sounded genuinely worried. "He would have been furious. Daddy says that he's a man of uncertain temper."

Casper looked at her, puzzled.

"What does that mean?"

"I'm not sure," Teddy admitted. "I think it means that he gets cross easily or something. But you shouldn't have done it, Casp. Anything might have happened."

Casper grinned.

"It was all right, he couldn't see me, I made sure of that. I was kneeling down under the window sill. He would have had to come over and look out. Anyway, I'd already thought about it. I can run faster than him."

Casper had a point there, thought Carlos. Sir William looked pretty fit and everything but there was no way he could catch a boy of Casper's age.

"So," continued Casper, "do you want to see it or not?"

He laid the phone back on the picnic table and without speaking Teddy and Carlos leaned in to look down at the screen. The unmistakeable face of Sir William Pelham came into view. He was sitting on a small wooden chair and sitting opposite him, her face turned away from the screen, sat a woman with long curly hair. Carlos felt suddenly tense. He had no idea what was coming next but whatever it was, he was getting the distinct feeling that it was something that he'd rather not hear. Sir William wasn't a man to be messed around with and the more miles there were between them, the better he liked it.

The woman spoke, her voice soft but clear. Teddy turned to Carlos, the surprise evident on her face.

"Carlos, that's Scarlett. It is. It's Scarlett." She looked confused. "What's Scarlett doing in there with Sir William?"

Casper reached across and turned the volume up.

"I'm warning you, Scarlett." Sir William's face held none of the genial character and charm that he usually presented to the world at large. Now it looked cold and threatening. Carlos felt a chill run through him. He wouldn't be in Scarlett's shoes. Not for anything.

"I know that you're involved in all this," Sir William continued. "Orlando told us, so don't waste your time trying to deny anything."

As he spoke, Scarlett stood up and walked across the room. She leaned with her back against the wall. The three teenagers could see her face clearly now. She was obviously scared but also, somehow, defiant. She stared back at Sir William.

"I'm doing you a favour, you know. I didn't have to come here to meet you."

Sir William smiled.

"Of course you didn't," he agreed, his tone pleasant but cool. "I could have just turned up at your house and confronted you in front of your parents. Or better still, I could have rung the police."

"What's the problem anyway?" Scarlett swept the hair from her face as she spoke. She looked, Carlos thought, very young with her hair pulled back like that. Not much older than himself really. He felt suddenly dreadfully sorry for her. However she had got herself into this mess, she clearly had no idea how she was going to get out of it. He listened harder as she continued. "You've got Orlando back. Nothing happened to him, and nothing would have happened to him. None of us would have hurt him."

Sir William looked triumphant.

"I knew it! You're not bloody bright enough to have managed it all on your own. So who else was involved in your sordid little plot?"

Scarlett stretched her face into a small sneer. You had to give it to her, thought Carlos. Terrified she might be, but she wasn't going to let herself be intimidated by him.

"Wouldn't you like to know?"

It was not, thought Carlos, the most mature response that she might have made but frankly he was impressed that she had managed to make any response at all. He suspected that if he had been in Scarlett's place he might not have been able to do the same. Sir William was exactly the kind of man who put the fear of God in him just by existing.

Sir William gave a grim smile.

"Yes, my dear. I would like to know. I would like to know very much indeed."

Suddenly, and without warning, he leapt from his chair and gripped her face in one large hand, pushing his thumb into her cheek and shoving her hard against the wall. Scarlett struggled against him, twisting her body this way and that until he released his grip. Sir William sat down again and folded his arms. Scarlett doubled over, trying to catch her breath.

"If I tell you," the words came out in short gasps as her breathing steadied, "will you let me go?"

Sir William thought for a moment.

"I might," he said at last.

"It was Bridie and Guido," said Scarlett. "They were in it together."

CHAPTER FORTY-TWO

SIR WILLIAM STARED at her. Scarlett laughed, a light brittle noise that rattled with bravado, a sound that was unconvincing to the ears of the listeners.

"They planned it all," she said. "They were going to go away together with the ransom money. The whole thing was a set-up." She walked back across the room and sat down again. They faced each other in silence.

"Your big mistake," continued Scarlett, leaning slightly forward and speaking quietly, "was to employ Guido. Bridie was at a dead end when you met, she told me so. When you turned up in the pub and kept bothering her she thought she'd won the jackpot. No more scratting around for acting jobs she wouldn't get, no more bar work or waitressing. She said that she decided that she'd play a bit hard to get, get you really interested, and then she'd reel you in. She said that it was like shooting fish in a barrel. She didn't even have to try very hard. After all, she was an actress." Scarlett smiled.

Sir William opened his mouth to speak and then closed it again.

"And then, once you were married," Scarlett spoke more confidently now, her voice growing stronger. "She got the house and the title and all the money she needed. The problem was, when she'd got all that, all she could see ahead of her was a lifetime of waiting for you to die. That was why she was so keen to start the hotel business. Apart from the fact that it gave her something to do, once you'd made her a director of the company and transferred some of your assets into the company name, she knew that whatever happened she would be all right. She had something of her own. And she enjoyed running the hotel. She had a couple of one-night flings with some of the guests you know," she added, almost as an afterthought.

Sir William swallowed hard but remained silent. In his heart, Carlos felt a pang of pity. It was bad enough that his wife was having an affair with one of his employees but apparently she had also been distributing her favours among the hotel guests. The very people that he greeted when they came down to breakfast. How they must have laughed behind his back. It wasn't the sort of thing that anybody wanted to hear about their partner but for a man of Sir William's pride and standing it must have been unbearable.

For several moments neither of them spoke.

"I asked her once why she didn't just divorce you," Scarlett said eventually.

"And what did she say?" Sir William's face remained impassive.

"She said that she didn't want to end up like the first Lady Pelham. And she said that she was bound to outlive you so she might just as well wait it out. She said that she'd get more that way."

"I see," said Sir William. "And how do I know that you're speaking the truth? What's so special about you that Bridie should take you into her confidence?"

"Oh, didn't you realise? We're cousins." Scarlett smirked. "We've known each other since I was a child. That's why when Guido and Bridie came up with the plan, they thought of me. They needed somebody on the inside, somebody that Orlando would trust. Of course, it couldn't be either of them, they needed to carry on as normal and play their parts. And I am a qualified nanny."

Scarlett settled back in her chair. She looked, thought Carlos, more relaxed now, although in Carlos's opinion that was a mistake. He suspected that people who crossed Sir William should never make the mistake of relaxing.

"I didn't take a lot of persuading," said Scarlett. "They offered me more money than I would ever make being a nanny." She looked thoughtful as she spoke, and slightly regretful. "So I gave in my notice to the family I was with and came to Seton Manor. If it had all worked, there would have been enough money for me to buy a little house and set up somewhere new. Maybe start my own nursery. All I had to do was take Orlando out of bed when the household was asleep and look after him for a few days."

Sir William nodded, his face grim.

"And Orlando didn't protest at being woken in the middle of the night? He just went with you?"

"Of course he just went with me. Orlando loved me. Anyway, I'd done a dummy run a couple of weeks earlier. It was Bridie's idea. I took him into the copse in the middle of the night and we toasted marshmallows over a little fire. I told him that it was a secret, that he mustn't ever tell anybody. Children are good at keeping secrets," she added.

Carlos felt slightly sick. Too good sometimes. He had heard too many tales from school and college friends about the jolly uncle or friendly partner of their mother who had made them keep secrets when they were little. Thank God that he'd had Maria. She had instilled in him from a very early age that if anybody, anybody at all, man, woman or child, tried to do anything to him that he felt uncomfortable with then he must shout out loud. Her voice, ringing back from beyond the grave, filled his head.

"Listen very carefully, Carlos. You must shout. Like this." And she had raised her head and screamed until his ears hurt and the birds dropped from the trees. "And also," she had added, "you must bite. Bite very hard." And she had gnashed her teeth together in a terrifying display of ferocity. Thankfully, he had never been called on to either scream or bite but it had been good advice. She had held him tight, hugging his tiny five year old body so close to her that he could feel her heart beating. "And if this person who is trying to do things to you then tells you that you must keep it a secret, then you must come straight to your mother. And she will kill this person."

She had smiled as she had said that last sentence but Carlos had the distinct feeling that she meant it. He listened harder as Scarlett continued.

"So I just told Orlando that we were going out to have another adventure. I took him down to the copse and we had marshmallows again and then I took him to Guido's apartment. He didn't know that it was Guido's. He'd never been in there before."

Sir William nodded again, his expression unaltered.

"I see. So what happened next?"

"I stayed in the apartment with him that night but I got up really early to make sure that I was back in my own room by the time that he was reported as missing. When everybody searched for him the next morning, Bridie and Guido made sure that they searched outside so that nobody would go near Guido's apartment. I had my story ready about needing to leave suddenly because of a family crisis but when you sacked me it actually made it all much easier. I just stayed with Orlando in the apartment. Guido had stocked up the fridge with food and if I wanted anything else I could always text Bridie. Guido stayed with a friend of Bridie's so that Orlando wouldn't see him. Bridie didn't want him to see her either," she added. "Just in case things went wrong."

"And, may I ask, did Bridie intend to take Orlando with her when she started this new life she had planned?"

"Oh yes. She's actually very fond of him you know. So am I. He's quite sweet when you get to know him. Guido said that they could all go to a place where you couldn't get at them."

"And where might that have been?" Sir William's eyes were like flint as he spoke.

"I don't know," Scarlett admitted. "Somewhere abroad, I think. Actually, I didn't really want to know. As soon as I got my money I wanted out."

Carlos watched as Sir William's face contorted in a grimace of pain, his fists clenching and unclenching. Not only had his adored wife planned to relieve him of large sums of money and flee the country with her lover, but she was going to take his beloved son with her.

"So why did you let him go?"

Scarlett took a deep breath.

"When Guido was found dead, I knew that it was all over. Guido was really the brains behind it all. He did the planning and everything, we just followed his instructions. Once he was gone, Bridie and me, well, we would never have managed on our own. Neither of us would have known where to start. Guido had lived in lots of different countries and knew loads of people, he was the one who was going to sort the money out and find them somewhere to live. So, after Bridie texted me that he was dead, I decided to leg it and leave the doors open so that Orlando could escape."

"And did you tell Bride that was what you intended to do?"

Scarlett shook her head.

"Not at first. At first we both just panicked. Neither of us really knew what to do. But I texted her back and met her later in the copse. We agreed that I should just go back to my parents and lie low for the present. She said to tell her when I was leaving and that she would go and collect Orlando. She said that she'd tell you that she'd heard him crying in the grounds or something. But then she didn't have to collect him because that boy found him."

"And it didn't occur to you that Orlando would tell us where he'd been? And who he'd been with?"

Scarlett nodded.

"Of course. Bride said that she would manage that. She said that she'd persuade you that Orlando was mistaken or making it up and that you shouldn't tell the police in case it upset him." She pulled a face. "My bad luck that you did believe him, I guess. To be honest, I think that at that point, neither of us was thinking straight. Anyway, she gave me some money to get further away. Actually, I was just looking up trains to London when you rang me."

"So why didn't you go then?" demanded Sir William.

"Because," said Scarlett simply, "I knew in my heart that you would find me, wherever I went. Or pay someone to find me."

"At least you're capable of making some sensible decisions," said Sir William. "What about the ransom demands? Who sent those?"

"Guido," said Scarlett. "He bought a cheap pay as you go and drove out into the countryside to send them."

Sir William remained silent. Scarlett tilted her head to one side and looked at him.

"I'm surprised that you didn't know about Bridie and Guido. They used to meet up after you went to bed you know. Bridie said that was one of the advantages of being married to an old man. You often went to bed early. She used to go over to Guido's apartment or meet him in the grounds. Really," she repeated, "I can't believe that you didn't know."

She looked at him, her expression quizzical.

"But perhaps you did know," she said softly. "Perhaps you did."

CHAPTER FORTY-THREE

TEDDY SAT ON the work surface and watched as Carlos rinsed out Aubrey and Vincent's food bowls and re-filled them before setting them back down. He straightened up and turned to face her.

"Where's Casper now?" he asked.

"In his bedroom. Sulking," she added.

"Teddy," Carlos spoke gently. He knew that Casper was upset but he'd had no choice but to take a stand when Casper had made the grand announcement that the Casper Beaumont International Detective Agency would henceforth be taking responsibility for investigating the death of Guido. "Teddy," he repeated. "No matter what Casper thinks, this isn't a game. It's all far too serious, and far too dangerous, for kids like us to be mucking about in it. We need to tell your father about it. He's a magistrate, he'll know what to do."

He didn't add, as he might have done, that the sooner they passed on the information they thought that they possessed to someone in authority, the safer they would be. He didn't want to frighten her, but his every instinct told him that Sir William was not a person to be trifled with, as his mother would have said. Actually, she had said made a trifle of but she meant the same thing.

Teddy jumped down and leaned over to stroke Aubrey.

"I know. You're right, of course. It's just well, you know, poor old Casp. He was so excited about it all." She looked up. "Shall we go and tell Daddy now?"

Carlos nodded.

"I think that we should. Might as well get it over with. Have you got Casper's mobile?"

Teddy pulled the phone out of her pocket and showed it to him.

"I made him give it to me. You don't think," she hesitated and then ploughed on. "You don't think that we might have got it all wrong? You know, that we've misunderstood or misinterpreted it or something?"

Carlos looked at her. No, he didn't think that they'd got it all wrong although it was so like Teddy to want to give the benefit of the doubt. But what else could Scarlett have meant when she had said that perhaps Sir William had known about Guido? And it was the way that she had said it, that soft slightly menacing tone that was unnerving even when listened to on a mobile phone. And the logical conclusion, the one to which all three of them had immediately jumped, was that if Sir William knew that Bridie and Guido were having an affair then that made him the obvious candidate for Guido's murder.

"Because if Sir William did know about Lady Pelham and Guido," continued Teddy, "why didn't he just sack Guido? Or divorce her or something? Why would he have to kill him?"

It was a good point, thought Carlos. Sir William genuinely loved Bridie. Or at least he was besotted with her, so it was probably unlikely that he'd want to divorce her. There was Orlando to consider too. If he divorced Bridie he might lose Orlando. Even in these enlightened times he knew for a fact that when a marriage broke down it was still nearly always the mother who got custody of the children. Quite a lot of his friends at college had parents who were divorced and he couldn't think of a single one who lived with their father. The mother had to be proved to be an unfit parent or something, although possibly Sir William could do that. After all, he was loaded. He could pay people to say whatever he wanted them to say. And, on reflection, it was true that Bridie had colluded with kidnapping her own son as well as having an affair with an employee so that didn't exactly qualify her for parent of the year.

But if Sir William was so mad about Bridie that he wouldn't divorce her, it came round to the same question. Why hadn't Sir William just sent Guido packing? He was the boss. He could have just given him a month's money and told him that he wasn't needed anymore. That kind of thing happened in the hospitality trade all the time, sometimes without the month's money. But, he supposed, even if Sir William had done that, it wouldn't have stopped Bridie seeing him. The only way to ensure that Bridie didn't see him was to remove him altogether.

He looked at Teddy and shrugged his shoulders.

"I don't know. But come on, let's go and see your dad. You'd better give Casper a shout to come down, too."

Aubrey lifted his head from his bowl and watched them go. He turned to Vincent and regarded him for a moment in silence.

"That night, Vin, you know, when they discovered that handy bloke's body in the pool, where did you go?"

Vincent lifted his head and blinked slowly.

"Out," he said.

Aubrey nodded.

"Did you see something?"

Vincent dipped his head back down to his food bowl and looked at Aubrey out of the corner of one eye.

"Like what?"

Aubrey suppressed a sigh. He loved Vincent dearly but he could be extremely annoying at times. But badgering him wouldn't get him anywhere. He took a deep breath.

"Did you see what happened by the pool?"

Vincent hesitated and then nodded slowly.

"Vin, why didn't you tell me?"

Vincent sat back and began washing his face, licking his paw and passing it across his ears in a slow rhythmic movement. Aubrey sat patiently and watched him. Washing was something that he often did himself while he thought about things. It bought a bit of time. Anyway, he could wait.

"That night," said Vincent eventually, "I was a bit restless so I went out. You were asleep on Carlos's bed so I didn't want to disturb you. Anyway, I went over to that old pigsty, you know, the one that we found. Just to have a look round. And then I saw him."

"Who? Vin, who did you see? Was it Guido or Sir William? Or someone else?"

"Sir William. He was walking really slowly and he had something sort of hanging over his arm." Vincent thought for a moment. "It was starting to get light and I decided to follow him. I don't know why really, it was just something to do."

Aubrey nodded.

"And then," Vincent continued, "he suddenly stopped and he took this thing off his arm and I could see then that it was a gun."

Aubrey nodded. He and Vincent knew about guns. They had both seen them before although fortunately they had never had one pointed at them. But the thing about a gun was that whoever held it, usually won the argument.

"He straightened it and sort of took a step back and then he fired it. And then there was a dead rabbit in front of him. I felt sorry for it but at least it was dead. At least it wasn't caught in a trap or anything."

Aubrey shivered slightly. They had both come across animals caught in traps before and there was nothing that you could do for them, except hope that death came sooner rather than later.

"Right." Aubrey thought for a moment. "So then what happened?"

"He just walked on so I carried on following him. He got as far as the apartments and that Guido bloke was there. He was by the pool." Vincent paused as he collected his thoughts. "Guido turned round," he continued, "and they both just sort of stood there."

"What did they say?" asked Aubrey.

"Nothing, to start with. They were just staring at each other and then Guido started laughing. Like as if he'd just been told a really good joke. And then Sir William walked right up to him and there was another loud bang and Guido fell in the pool."

"Vin, why didn't you tell me?" Aubrey repeated. "Why did you keep it to yourself."

And as he looked in his friend's eyes he saw a flicker of anxiety reflected back at him. Vincent hadn't told him because he wanted to pretend that he hadn't seen it. That everything was normal, that there was nothing to rock the boat. That if he didn't speak about it then it hadn't happened and everything would just carry on as normal. Aubrey felt his heart squeeze. Vincent's coolness of character was really just a mask. Vincent was as vulnerable as the next cat. Perhaps even more so.

They had never really spoken about the tragic death of Vincent's previous owners and Aubrey had assumed that Vincent had come to terms with it. But now he thought about it, Vincent had never told him how he had come to be separated from his first owner either. She had been an elderly lady who had, he had told Aubrey, cooked fresh fish for him every Friday night and had let it cool before flaking it into a bowl for him. Perhaps she had died, he now thought. Or had to go into one of those human catteries or something, somewhere where they wouldn't allow people to bring their pets. Whatever the truth of the matter, Vincent had, like him, ended up in a rescue centre before being picked by another family. And if things ever went wrong with the Goodmans, that's where they'd both end up again. That's if they were lucky. But, he thought, suddenly cheering up, right now all was well in their world. They had Molly, Jeremy and Carlos. And they had each other.

"Shove over, fatso," he said. "Give us a chance to get at the food."

CHAPTER FORTY-FOUR

EMILY LOOKED UP as her father entered the room. He looked as though he had aged about ten years over the last few days. The lines on his face had deepened and his skin held an unhealthy pallor. His thick grey hair, usually so stylishly well-cut, had grown too long so that it hung in wispy little strands over the back of his collar. While some ageing rock stars could undoubtedly get away with such a look, it made Sir William appear haggard and slightly disreputable. Like the kind of man that you edged away from at a party. Next to her, Edward laid aside the book that he had been pretending to read and waited for his father to speak. In the chair opposite Jacob sat and stared into space, deep in thought. For several minutes nobody spoke, the only sound was that of one of house-keeping staff vacuuming the stairs. It was, thought Emily, an oddly comforting noise. At least some semblance of normality was being maintained.

"Father," said Edward, breaking the silence at last. "What's happening? What's going on? Have they let you go?"

Sir William shook his head.

"No, Edward, they have not. I am still in what I believe is called custody But they are at least letting me have a little private time with the three of you. There are things that I wish to speak to you about."

Jacob blinked and transferred his gaze to his father.

"Father, what is all this about? I mean, surely, it can't be true?"

Sir William nodded and passed his hands over his eyes before speaking. His voice, when it came, was grave and slow.

"I'm afraid that it is, Jacob."

Emily felt a sudden urge to rush from the room, to push her fingers into her ears and escape from whatever was coming next. Ever since the police cars had drawn up on the drive and the officers had entered the morning room and confronted her father, it had felt like some sort of surreal nightmare. They had listened, aghast, as not only had the police officers stated their intention to question her father about the murder of Guido but he had admitted it before they had even had a chance to get into their stride. She and Jacob and Edward had stood rooted to the spot, numb with shock and unable to speak, as calmly, quietly, their father had confessed to the murder of another human being. At his request, the officers had followed him through to his study, leaving his three elder children stunned with disbelief.

"Where are the police now?" asked Emily.

"Waiting for me in the hall," replied Sir William, his tone calm and measured. "I have asked the kitchen staff to bring them coffee if they wish it."

Edward stared at him and struggled for a moment to smother the burst of laughter that was threatening to erupt. Any minute now his father was going to be arrested for murder, if he hadn't been already, but he was still behaving as though he was the lord of the manor. Although, he reflected, what else was he supposed to do? At least it gave him some dignity, some sense of being in control. And being in control was the one thing that he had always been. Until now. He took a deep breath and pressed his lips firmly together. Whatever else happened, now was definitely not the time to start laughing. He didn't even think that it was funny, not in the slightest. He was, he knew, on the edge. He could feel the chilly fingers of hysteria creeping over his brain, pulling out his rational thoughts and starting to unravel them, but he must hold on. He must keep himself in check. The events of the morning, piled on top of the strain that he was already under, was pushing him to the brink but for the sake of his father he needed to remain calm and composed. He threw a quick glance across at Emily. She appeared on the verge of tears.

"I think that there must be some mistake, Father," said Jacob, leaning forward, his hands clasped together and his voice unusually gentle. "Some sort of mix up. Somebody has obviously got hold of the wrong end of the stick somewhere along the line." He turned to his brother. "Ed, surely you can speak to one of the partners at your practice. Obviously, there must be some rational explanation, some…"

Sir William held up his hand and smiled thinly at his son.

"Your faith in me is touching, Jacob. But there is no mistake."

"But Daddy, it can't be true, I mean…" Emily began, floundering, groping for the right words and failing, before subsiding into silence. Perhaps their father was confused, she thought, perhaps he didn't know what he was saying. Perhaps this was the onset of some dreadful disease. But confusion wasn't a characteristic that he had ever displayed before, and he didn't appear to be displaying it now.

Sir William sat down on the sofa and regarded his three children.

"It is true that I murdered Guido." He paused and swallowed before continuing. "He was having an affair with Bridie."

Emily's fingers flew to her mouth, her face frozen in shock.

"How did you find out?" asked Jacob and then instantly regretted asking the question. In the circumstances, it wasn't the most sensitive thing that he could have said. While his relationship with his father hadn't always been of the best, his instinct now was to protect him. He certainly had no wish to hurt him any further.

Sir William raised one eyebrow as he turned to his eldest son.

"Quite by chance. Which, I suppose, is often the way with these things."

He sighed and stood up again. Reaching over towards the mantlepiece, he picked up the small silver frame which held the picture of himself and Bridie on their wedding day. He, tall and dignified in his beautifully cut suit and silk waistcoat, looking down at her with pride. She, in her pretty pale blue lace dress with the diamonds he had given her sparkling around her neck, gazing adoringly up at him. Their hands were intertwined. He stared down at it, his expression unfathomable, before replacing it and looking back up at his children.

"One night," he continued, "I awoke in the early hours and Bridie was missing from our bed. I thought that she may have been unable to sleep and was perhaps sitting downstairs, reading or watching television. I got up and looked for her but she was nowhere to be seen, so I wondered if perhaps she had taken herself out for a walk. I was worried about her being out there in the dark on her own so I set off to find her." His face twisted slightly at the irony of the thought of Bridie being out in the dark on her own. "And I saw them. In the copse. As naked as the day they were born. At first I thought it was a couple of villagers, trespassing. But as I moved closer I could see them clearly. They obviously didn't see me. Which was not surprising. They were otherwise occupied."

"Poor Daddy," said Emily, her voice soft. "How dreadful for you."

And, she suddenly realised, she meant it. Much as she disliked Bridie, much as she had secretly, and sometimes not so secretly, wished that her father's second marriage would end, he was still her father and she still loved him. To see him brought so low, and by that money-grabbing, mean-spirited little bitch, hurt her more than she would have thought possible.

"I decided at first," continued Sir William, as if Emily hadn't spoken, "to simply ignore it, to turn a blind eye. It was, I confess, the easy option but I also hoped, you see, that it would just fizzle out. That she would get bored with him and come to her senses. After all, what could he give her? Having lived the life that she had at Seton Manor, I thought it unlikely that she would settle for anything less. At least, not in the long term."

"Why didn't you get rid of him?" asked Edward. "You could have just sacked him."

"Because I was afraid that if she was sufficiently infatuated she would leave with him. And if she did that then of course she might take Orlando with her. I tried not to think about it, to push it out of my mind, and for the most part I succeeded. Then of course Orlando went missing and finding him became my priority."

Sir William paused for a moment and then continued.

"I was even fool enough to think that, dreadful though the kidnapping of Orlando was, in a strange way it might have brought us closer together again. That she would forget Guido in her anxiety about our son."

"So what happened with Guido?" asked Jacob. "Was it an accident or something?"

Sir William shook his head.

"No, Jacob. It was not an accident."

"Do you want to tell us about it?" Edward spoke gently, he felt calmer now the first shock of the morning's revelations had passed. For the first time, he realised, he felt a real sense of compassion for his father, an understanding of what he had been through. After all, wasn't he also facing an impossible situation? And, like his father, was it not a situation brought about by his determination, his absolute need, to keep his wife by his side at all costs?

CHAPTER FORTY-FIVE

SIR WILLIAM GLANCED out of the window. Outside the two dogs were playing on the lawn, each of them pulling at what looked like an old wellington boot. For a moment he was distracted. Where had they got the boot, he wondered? It had better not be one of the gardener's. He would never hear of the end of it.

"Father?" said Edward quietly.

Sir William blinked and brought himself back to the present. He looked at each of his three children in turn. He felt suddenly rather proud of them. They were taking things remarkably calmly. There had been no hysterics, no condemnation. They had simply listened. Perhaps they were more like him than he had thought.

"I'm sorry, Edward. Yes. I think that it's right that you should know before it hits the papers. I would far rather that you heard the truth directly from me rather than some sensationalised drivel in the press. In fact, it's rather a relief to talk about it." Sir William spoke slowly, measuring out his words. "I had been sleeping badly for several nights," he began, and then stopped.

It was hardly surprising, thought Emily. His youngest son had been kidnapped and his wife was having an affair with one of his employees. It would have been enough to drive most men completely over the edge. It was a testament to her father's strength of character that he had presented the same unchanged face to the world, that there had been absolutely no hint of the inner turmoil that he must have been suffering. She gave a small smile of encouragement. Sir William cleared his throat and began again.

"I had been sleeping badly," he repeated. "On that particular morning I woke early, just before day break. I need hardly say that it was a matter of some relief that Bridie was asleep next to me." His eyes took on a remote, unfocused, look as though he was remembering something from long ago and far away. "I was thinking of what to do about Orlando, whether or not to go the police or to hire a private detective to find him. My instinct was that the whole business had a distinctively amateur feel to it, that these were not professional kidnappers that we were dealing with. And I wasn't sure whether that made matters better or worse. Better, I supposed, in that they would be easier to deal with. Worse, in that they might panic and cause real harm to Orlando."

He stared down at his hands for a moment, turning them palm upwards and studying the lines. He looked, thought Emily, as though he was telling his own fortune. And perhaps he was.

"So I decided that the best thing to do, rather than just lay there worrying, was to get up and take a walk to clear my head and while I was about it I thought that I would bag a few rabbits. The gardener had told me that the rascals had got into the lettuces again." He cleared his throat before continuing. "I collected my gun from the gun room and headed out. I walked about for a bit, thinking, trying to make up my mind about what to do, and then I saw him, Guido, by the pool, cleaning it ready for the guests."

The silence in the room was almost palpable. Emily, Edward and Jacob leaned forward.

"What happened next, Father?" asked Jacob.

Sir William paused while he gathered his thoughts again before continuing.

"I stood for a moment and watched as he leaned over the pool. He looked so young and so strong. He seemed to radiate vigour. In fact, he reminded me of myself in my younger days, something about the way he moved and the set of his shoulders. He must have sensed that I was there because he stood up and turned and faced me. For several seconds neither of us said anything. And then the swine threw back his head and laughed at me. He just stood there, laughing. So I unhooked my gun, walked right up to him, and shot him."

"What did you do then?" asked Edward.

Sir William gave a slight shrug.

"I could see that the fellow was dead. Or, if he wasn't, he soon would be. I would like to say that I felt some regret, but I didn't. The man had stolen my wife. He had made a fool of me." Sir William's mouth tightened. "So, in answer to your question Edward, I simply went back to the house and carried on as normal. It seemed to me to be the best thing to do."

"Did Bridie know?" asked Emily.

Sir William shook his head.

"No. I told nobody. For obvious reasons," he added wryly. "Bridie may have suspected. In fact I rather think that she did, but she said nothing."

"Actually," said Edward. "Where is Bridie?"

"Bridie has left Seton Manor," said Sir William. "She left first thing this morning and she will not be returning."

"Why? Where has she gone?"

Emily looked from her father to her brothers, the confusion stamped on her face. If anybody knew when they were on to a good thing, then surely it was Bridie. Why on earth would she walk away from it? And with Guido out of the picture, where would she go? She had never heard Bridie mention any family. Or, indeed, any close friends now she thought about it.

"She has left at my request," Sir William replied. "I informed her last night that my intention is to divorce her. I have further informed her that if she attempts to thwart me in any way then she will live to regret it."

"But Daddy, I thought, I mean, surely .."

She looked at her two brothers. They looked as puzzled as she did. Their father had just told them that he had loved Bride so much that, unbelievable as it seemed, given what they knew of his character, he had been prepared to overlook her infidelity. Why was he suddenly talking about divorcing her? What had she done? She felt her head swim. Everything today had turned upside down.

CHAPTER FORTY-SIX

JACOB GOT UP and walked over to the window, his heart heavy. Whatever the situation with Bridie, his father was going to prison that was for sure. He watched as the two dogs continued to enjoy their tug of war with the wellington boot, their ears back and their feathery tails flying What would happen to them now, he thought. They were such lovely creatures. The thought of them going to a rescue centre, or even worse, being destroyed, was unbearable. Perhaps he could take them? After all, given his employment status, it wasn't like they would be left alone all day. He turned back as Emily spoke again.

"Father, what has Bridie done? I mean, apart from…" She hesitated. "I mean apart from…"

It was no good. She couldn't bring herself to say it.

Sir William gave a small smile.

"You mean apart from engaging in a sexual relationship with the handyman?"

Emily nodded miserably. She hadn't meant to rub it in.

"When Orlando informed us of Scarlett's involvement with his kidnapping," said Sir William, "Bridie was most insistent that he had invented it, that he was making up stories, and initially, briefly, I believed that to be the case. Children often confuse reality with fantasy. It is part of the charm of childhood." He smiled suddenly. "You for instance, Jacob, were always convinced that there was a unicorn living in your wardrobe."

Jacob stared at him. It was true. When he was about three years old, he had shared his bedroom with an imaginary unicorn. He'd forgotten all about it. And his father had always made a point of opening the wardrobe door and saying goodnight to it. He felt his throat thicken.

"However," Sir William continued. "I was not entirely convinced. Orlando is a prosaic child, unlike the three of you. He is not normally given to flights of fancy. So I thought that it could do no harm to question Scarlett. At the very least, she might have seen or heard something on the night that Orlando disappeared that would help us. I tracked her down to her parents' house and insisted that she meet me."

"What did she say?" asked Jacob. "Did she admit it?"

Sir William nodded.

"Oh yes, she admitted it. She also provided me with the names of her co-conspirators."

"And?" breathed Emily, although, in a flash of insight, she thought that she knew the answer before it came.

"Bridie and Guido. The whole thing was a plot to relieve me of a large amount of money so that they could go off together, and the plan was that they would take Orlando with them. While I could forgive the occasional infidelity, I could not forgive the magnitude of the deceit or the intention to deprive me of my son."

"Where has she gone?" asked Jacob.

Sir William shrugged.

"I neither know nor care. I have made such financial arrangements as to ensure that she has sufficient to live on. She will not want for anything. After all, she does bear out family name and she is the mother of my youngest son, although whether she is fit to carry that title is another matter entirely."

Edward looked at his father's face. What he was seeing, he knew, was a man who had well and truly fallen out of love. And there was nothing so icy cold as a love that had died. His father would, he knew, show no weakness. Unlike his treatment of his mother, he suddenly realised. While his father may have become bored in his marriage and had fallen into the age old trap of being an older man seeking a younger wife in order to reinvigorate himself, he hadn't, Edward thought, ever really born any animosity towards his first wife. If anything, depending on how you looked at it, he had taken care of her. He certainly hadn't banished her from his sight.

Sir William cleared his throat and stood slightly taller. Emily felt her heart give a tiny squeeze. What it must have cost him to demonstrate his weaknesses in front of his children. Or in front of anybody.

"I have made it clear to Bridie," said Sir William, "that I will not engage in any attempt to make any further claim on me. If she tries any such thing, I will ensure that she will never see Orlando again. I spoke to my solicitors yesterday and they have already started divorce proceedings on my behalf, which she will not contest. Likewise, the custody of Orlando will not be an issue."

Edward looked at his father, the admiration clear on his face. You had to give it to the old man. Even now, even when he was on the precipice of losing not only his freedom but his reputation and everything that he had worked so hard for, he was endeavouring to speak with the same assured certainty that he always had. Just as he had the time when Edward, aged seven, had been hit on the face by a stone thrown by one of the village boys which had cut his cheek. He closed his eyes as he recalled the comforting weight of his father's hand on his shoulder. 'You must forget all about it, Edward. The boy will not bother you again.' And he hadn't.

"Where is Orlando now?" asked Edward.

"Playing in his room. One of the village girls is looking after him. I have engaged her on a temporary basis."

"What are you going to do about him in the long term?" asked Jacob. "What's going to happen to him? Who's going to look after him?"

"Orlando will remain here at Seton Manor," said Sir William. "It is his home."

"But Daddy," Emily faltered. Did her father not realise the terrible trouble that he was in? How could he possibly think that, having just confessed to murder, he could keep Orlando here? Surely to God he wasn't going to employ another nanny and then just leave Orlando here with her? What if she walked out or neglected him or something? None of the domestic staff lived in. What if she went out for the night? He'd be left in Seton Manor on his own. He was just a child. Anything could happen. She felt no particular fondness for Orlando but he was still her flesh and blood, and she certainly wouldn't want anything to happen to him. But then, what was the alternative other than to place him in care? Her father had no brothers or sisters so there were no aunts or uncles to step in, no cousins to lend a hand.

Sir William laughed, a small ripple of amusement that lightened his features and made him look suddenly like his old self.

"Don't look so tragic, Emily. I have, of course, thought this through very carefully. I was very well aware that it would probably only be a matter of time before somebody joined the dots in relation to Guido's murder."

He tipped his head to one side and regarded his children.

"You think, all three of you, that I am entirely ruthless. That I think only of myself. No, don't deny it." He held up his hand as Edward opened his mouth to speak. "You think that I treated your mother very badly and, in truth, I think that I would agree with you. All things considered, she deserved better. I have been a fool. And what is worse, I have been an old fool. But my decision to house your mother in the estate cottage was for her benefit you know, not mine. If Bridie had her way, your mother would have been packed off to Australia. But I could see the level at which she was drinking and I could see also that it was growing steadily worse. At least if she was nearby I could keep an eye on her. I could make sure that she had a roof over her head and that all her bills were paid. There seemed little point in making her a greater allowance, she would have simply drunk it away and died an even earlier death."

Emily stared at her father. His words had the undeniable ring of truth. She felt suddenly ashamed that none of them had ever considered that her mother's welfare might be of concern to their father, heavy-handed though that concern might have been. None of them had ever given him the benefit of the doubt, not once. From their perspective, he had simply fallen for a much younger woman and had wasted no time in getting rid of their mother. And, much as she hated to admit it, even to herself, their mother had been drinking too much for years, long before Bridie came on the scene. They had all known it. She pushed away the sudden memory of the morning of her eighteenth birthday and her mother stumbling on the stairs as she came down to breakfast, her words slurring as she wished her daughter many happy returns of the day. They had, all of them, turned a blind eye to the problem.

"You may not think so, but I was deeply saddened by Elizabeth's death," Sir William continued. "We were married for many years and I have no doubt that she was a loyal wife. Unlike the second Lady Pelham," he added.

Jacob, Edward and Emily remained silent.

"You think also that I know nothing of your current circumstances." Sir William sighed. "Emily, I am very well aware of the financial difficulties that you are in and that the shop has not paid its way for some time. You appear to have forgotten that I am a signatory to both your business and your personal accounts and as such am entitled to check the state of your finances at any time. Which, of course, I have done on a regular basis."

CHAPTER FORTY-SEVEN

EMILY SWALLOWED. He was right. She had forgotten. At the time it had seemed like a mere formality. But, of course, his name was on the cheque book. The cheque book that lay gathering dust in her desk drawer because, who used cheque books anymore? And she had long since given up looking at bank statements. They just depressed her.

"Daddy, I…" she began and then stopped. What could she say? He'd seen the financial state that she was in. There was no point in pretending or trying to make any excuses.

Sir William sat beside her and took her hand, turning it over and patting her palm as he spoke.

"Emily, there is no need for explanation. It is hard enough at any time to make a business pay. I, of all people, should know that. And I blame myself for encouraging you and also for not stepping in sooner. I think I believed that, given enough time, you would turn the situation around. However, I am forced to accept that while you have many excellent qualities, you are not a woman of business and I should have acknowledged that."

He let go of Emily's hand and turned to his eldest son.

"Jacob, I heard at the club about the redundancies in the civil service and made it my business to investigate further. It didn't take me long to discover that your department was for the axe. Several members of parliament are also members of my club and they were disappointingly willing to give me the information that I sought."

Jacob remained silent. Sir William looked at Edward, the most sensitive of his children and, in some ways, the most vulnerable. He was also the one who most closely resembled his mother.

"As for you Edward, I must confess that I am not entirely sure what trouble you have managed to get yourself into but, given the nature of your profligate wife and your astonishingly high standard of living, I imagine that it involves money. And given the nature of your employment, I also imagine that the money involved was not yours to spend?"

Edward nodded miserably, unable to speak. Any desire to laugh had drained away completely.

Sir William stood up and helped himself to a generous measure from the whisky decanter that stood on top of the console table.

"Might as well while I still can."

He took a long appreciative swallow and looked fondly at his three elder children.

"Cheer up. I am not the hard-hearted man that you think I am. But neither am I a fool. Although recent events might suggest otherwise." He pulled his mouth down in a mock grimace. "Of course, I always had every intention of helping you out although I had decided not to make it too easy for you. However, given the current circumstances, there seems to me to be no point in dragging matters out any further. Emily, if you agree, we will sell the shop and pay the debts. Then I would like you to live at Seton Manor and look after Orlando until my return. I shall, of course, pay you a decent allowance."

Emily felt a delightfully cooling sense of relief trickle through her. Her father was offering her a lifeline and she knew it. All the weight of recent months fell away and she felt suddenly light-headed. All right, she would have to care for the odious Orlando but what was that compared to the freedom that she was now being offered? Anyway, once she had Orlando to herself she might be able to change him. She thought rapidly. For a start, she would cut out all those sweets and bars of chocolate and persuade him to eat some decent food. She would get rid of those dreadful sailor suits that Bridie had insisted on dressing him in. She would dress him in shorts and T shirts like other children wore. And she would also enrol him at the village school ready for his next birthday. It was about time that he started mixing with ordinary people.

Sir William drained his glass and re-filled it before turning to his eldest son.

"As for you, Jacob, I rather thought that in my enforced absence, you might care to run the hotel? I would be sorry to let it go after putting so much work into it. You undoubtedly have highly developed administrative and managerial skills and I think that you would make an excellent job of taking it into the future. Unless you have other plans, of course."

Jacob stared at his father. He was a civil servant, through and through. It was all he had ever known. He had certainly never considered himself in the position of hotelier before. But the more he thought about it, the more attractive a proposition it appeared to be. It couldn't be more difficult than running a government department anyway. And there'd be no office politics to contend with, no more jockeying for position, no more worrying about the rumour mill. And as for Felicity, she could join him or not as she chose. If she chose not, he could still see the children. In fact, they might very well enjoy visiting Seton Manor. He would ensure that all the facilities were available to them. It would be like giving them little holidays. In the long term it would probably bring them closer to him.

"It is my intention," Sir William continued, "to dissolve the current company of which Seton Manor forms part of the assets, and establish a new one. I shall make you managing director."

Jacob stood up and held out his hand to his father.

"Father, I would be delighted."

"Excellent." Sir William sipped at his whisky.

"Father," said Edward. "What about me?"

"Ah yes, Edward." Sir William looked at his son thoughtfully. "What about you, indeed? I have, naturally, given the matter some thought. Unlike Emily and Jacob, my feeling is that you would not like a change of lifestyle. Therefore, I intend to give you sufficient money to extricate yourself from whatever trouble that you are in. On the proviso, however, that you at least make some attempt to reign in your wife's spending habits."

"Father," said Edward, unable to stop the smile from spreading across his face. "I really don't know how to thank you."

"There is no need, Edward," said Sir William. "Now to practicalities. I have instructed my solicitors to advance each of you such money as you need and to proceed with the sale of the shop. Emily and Jacob, you may move in to Seton Manor as soon as you wish. Emily, with regard to Orlando, I ask only that you do not tell him the truth about his mother. No doubt he will find out at some point but there is only so much reality that a five year old can deal with. I would also prefer that you did not bring him to visit me in prison although I would appreciate regular updates and photographs. I don't mind what story you tell him, as long as you are kind to him."

"Of course, Daddy," said Emily.

"I am hoping," said Sir William, "that my detention at Her Majesty's pleasure will not be for too long. I shall, of course, have the best counsel to speak for me."

"Daddy," Emily spoke slowly. "Why did you tell the police that you did it? Why didn't you just say nothing and let them prove it?"

"Because, my dear Emily," replied Sir William. "I am a pragmatist. I realised immediately that if they wanted to question me about the death of Guido then they must know about his affair with Bridie. By pleading guilty, I shall avoid the painful experience of a trial."

Emily suddenly jumped up and threw her arms around her father, joined instantly by Jacob and Edward.

Sir William looked astonished and then laughed.

"I believe that we are having what is called a group hug."

CHAPTER FORTY-EIGHT

THE SUMMER SEEMED a long time ago now, there was a faint chill in the air and the nights were drawing in. One of the neighbours had lit an early evening bonfire and the tang of smoke drifted across the gardens towards him. Carlos reached across and closed the window, glancing across at the photograph that he had taken of Teddy at the cricket match as he did so. Enlarged and framed now in a pretty painted frame that Molly had given to him, he had placed it carefully on the wall opposite his bed. Unbeknown to her, he had held on to the daisies when he had helped her untangle the chain which she had made for her hair and it rested now, dried and fragile, in the special drawer where he kept his mother's rosary.

He moved across to his bed and smoothed his hands across the duvet and pillows. Teddy would be calling any minute now and he didn't want her to see his unmade bed in the background. He turned and straightened up as the sound of his mobile trilled into the room. Leaping to his desk, he touched the screen of his phone and smiled as Teddy's pretty face appeared. She smiled back at him, making her tiny dimples twinkle and her eyes sparkle.

"How was your first day back at college?" she asked.

"All right. Mostly just getting timetables and that. A bit boring really. We were only in until lunchtime. We didn't have any actual classes. How was yours?"

"Ok, fine. Like yours, sorting timetables and stuff. Strange to think that this is our last year."

Carlos nodded. She was right, there was something strange about it. By this time next year they would be grown-ups. Officially adult. It didn't seem real somehow. Maybe it would be all right when it happened, he thought. Things usually were.

"Emily Pelham came to see us at the weekend," Teddy continued. "Mummy invited her for lunch and she brought Orlando with her. She told Mummy that Bridie had put his name down for some posh pre-prep school but Emily said that she was going to put a stop to that. She's going to enrol him in the village school. She said that would need to speak to the Head about how to handle it though."

"How to handle what? Orlando going to school?"

Teddy shook her head.

"No. You know, about Sir William and all that. She wants to try to make sure that Orlando doesn't get picked on or anything because of what his father did." She paused for a moment. "You know that Sir William was sent to prison?"

Carlos nodded. He did know. At the time of the trial, it had been in all the papers, and on television too. Millionaire businessman pleaded guilty to murdering faithless wife's lover, with unflattering shots of Sir William being herded from prison vans and into court. The monster that he had created of Sir William had turned into a shambling figure with his head under a blanket. But, on balance, he didn't think that Orlando would suffer too many problems at school. His own experience of notoriety when his mother had been killed had resulted in him being more popular, not less. Some of the girls at school had even wanted to take selfies with him. Anyway, Sir William Pelham was loaded and in his experience of life that went a long way. He couldn't see the parents of the village children not allowing their sons and daughters to play with Orlando or visit Seton Manor.

"Daddy said that he'd got off lightly, considering what he did," continued Teddy. "He said that he must have had a really good team of barristers."

"Well, he didn't get off that lightly really," pointed out Carlos. "Not when you think about it. He was still sent to prison."

"Yes, but not for life," said Teddy. "They reduced the charge to manslaughter, Daddy told us. It was because his lawyers told the court that he didn't really mean it, that Guido wound him up or something."

Carlos looked shocked. You couldn't go around killing people just because somebody wound you up. On that basis, half of the kids at Sir Frank's wouldn't have lived to see their fifteenth birthday.

"It's some law thing," said Teddy. "You still have to go to prison, just not for life. And he's really old so they'll probably let him out early anyway."

Carlos nodded. Really, he didn't care one way or the other.

"Actually, Orlando isn't as bad as we thought," said Teddy, changing the subject.

"Really?"

Carlos sounded doubtful. Although, he supposed, it was all relative. Orlando not being as bad as they had thought probably just meant that he hadn't actually thrown a tantrum or damaged anything while visiting the Beaumonts.

"No, honestly, really. He was dressed in proper jeans and a T shirt, not those stupid suit things he used to wear and Emily has had his hair cut properly. He looked quite normal. Casper took him out to play in the garden."

"What?" Carlos was astonished. Why would Casper take Orlando out to play in the garden?

Teddy laughed.

"Between you and me, Casper has decided that he needs an apprentice for his detective agency and that Orlando Pelham is just the boy for the job. Casper reckons that he ought to start training him now so that he's ready when the agency opens properly."

Carlos laughed.

"So what training did he do?"

"Casper hid some fruit around the garden in little plastic bags, pieces of banana and strawberries and some raspberries, and then challenged Orlando to find them. And he timed him so he had to run. Emily Pelham was well impressed. She said that she's going to try that at home. Oh, and before I forget," Teddy continued, "Mummy said to ask you if you would like to come and stay for a few days over half-term?"

Carlos tried, and failed, to look nonchalant.

DOWNSTAIRS IN THE kitchen, Aubrey and Vincent lay draped across the top of their cat domes, squashing them down flat while they listened contentedly to Molly and Jeremy. This was Aubrey's favourite time of the day, when they were all together and the front door was firmly closed to the outside world.

"No, honestly Moll, I'm sure that he's fine," said Jeremy, leaning back against the work surface and pulling the cork from a bottle of wine. "He's up in his room now, talking to Teddy. He's barely mentioned it since we've been home."

"I'm expect that you're right," said Molly. "It was just, you know, given all the reports in the papers and so on, I was worried that it would, well, remind him I suppose…"

They both fell silent for a moment. Aubrey knew what they were thinking. When Carlos's mother had died, that had been all over the press too. And try as they might, Molly and Jeremy hadn't always been able to turn off the television in time or hide the newspapers as the dreadful story unfolded.

"Anyway," said Jeremy. "He seems okay so let's not trouble trouble until trouble troubles us, as my grandmother used to say. This is his last year at college so let's hope that it goes smoothly." He poured a glass of wine and passed it to Molly. "Anyway, it'll be Christmas before we know it. And I suggest that we have a nice quiet time at home. No drama. No murders. Just a nice quiet Christmas."

ACKNOWLEDGEMENTS

Enormous appreciation, as always, for the enthusiasm, support and encouragement of Sean Coleman and his team at Red Dog Press, also to my new friends at Bloodhound Books who have supported the Cat Noir series with such positivity.

A big thank you to my fellow authors at Red Dog Press who are generous, talented and kind, and exactly the sort of people to share a kennel with.

ABOUT THE AUTHOR

I was born in London and spent my teenage years in Hertfordshire where I spent large amounts of time reading novels, watching daytime television and avoiding school.

Failing to gain any qualifications in science whatsoever, the dream of being a forensic scientist collided with reality when a careers teacher suggested that I might like to work in a shop. I don't think she meant Harrods.

Later studying law, I decided to teach rather than go into practice and have spent many years teaching mainly criminal law and criminology to young people and adults.

I enjoy reading crime novels, doing crosswords, and drinking wine. Not necessarily in that order.

Printed in Great Britain
by Amazon

12906708R00150